BOOK 10

THE DEMONATA

HELL'S HEROES

BY DARREN SHAN

LITTLE, BROWN AND COMPANY
New York   Boston

Little, Brown and Company

Hachette Book Group
237 Park Avenue, New York, NY 10017
Visit our website at www.lb-teens.com

Little, Brown and Company is a division of Hachette Book Group, Inc.
The Little, Brown name and logo are trademarks of Hachette Book Group, Inc.

The publisher is not responsible for websites (or their content)
that are not owned by the publisher.

First U.S. Paperback Edition: July 2011
First U.S. Hardcover Edition: May 2010
First published in Great Britain by Collins in 2009

The characters and events portrayed in this book are fictitious. Any similarity to real persons, living or dead, is coincidental and not intended by the author.

Library of Congress Cataloging-in-Publication Data

Shan, Darren.
Hell's heroes / by Darren Shan. — 1st ed.
p. cm. — (Demonata ; bk. 10)
Summary: Bec, Kernel, and Grubbs gear up for the fight of their lives as the final battle between Earth and the hordes of the Demonata draws near.
ISBN 978-0-316-04895-8 (hc) / ISBN 978-0-316-04891-0 (pb)
[1. Demonology—Fiction. 2. Magic—Fiction. 3. Werewolves—Fiction.
4. Horror stories.] I. Title.
PZ7.S52823Hel 2010
[Fic]—dc22
2009045626

10 9 8 7 6 5 4 3 2 1

RRD-C

Printed in the United States of America

OTHER TITLES AVAILABLE FROM
DARREN SHAN:

Birth of a Killer BOOK 1
Ocean of Blood BOOK 2

THE THIN EXECUTIONER

A Living Nightmare BOOK 1
The Vampire's Assistant BOOK 2
Tunnels of Blood BOOK 3
Vampire Mountain BOOK 4
Trials of Death BOOK 5
The Vampire Prince BOOK 6
Hunters of the Dusk BOOK 7
Allies of the Night BOOK 8
Killers of the Dawn BOOK 9
The Lake of Souls BOOK 10
Lord of the Shadows BOOK 11
Sons of Destiny BOOK 12

THE DEMONATA
Lord Loss BOOK 1
Demon Thief BOOK 2
Slawter BOOK 3
Bec BOOK 4
Blood Beast BOOK 5
Demon Apocalypse BOOK 6
Death's Shadow BOOK 7
Wolf Island BOOK 8
Dark Calling BOOK 9
Hell's Heroes BOOK 10

✠ ✠ ✠

For:
Liam, Bidely, and Bas — the Father, the Mother, and
the Holy Bust!!!

OBEs (Order of the Bloody Entrails) to:
Geir, Wiedar, Jon, and all the other nocturnal
Norwegian Shan crew

Road Managers:
Geraldine Stroud — the ripper skipper!
Mary Byrne — the tipsy first mate!

Editor-in-chief:
Stella Paskins — 10 rounds, not out!!

Apocalyptic Agents:
the Christopher Little chorus line

And an extra-special thank-you to all of my demonically delightful
Shansters, especially those of you who have kept me company on
the Web through the run of the series. But take heed — if you
desert me at this point, heads will roll!!!!

✠ ✠ ✠

THE LAST LAUGH

✛ ✛ ✛

I miss Cal," Dervish says. "We fought a lot when we were young, like all brothers, but we were always there for one another."

We're lying in the mouth of a cave, admiring the desolate desert view, sheltered from the fierce afternoon sun.

"It's funny," Dervish chuckles. "I thought I'd be the first to go. The life I chose, the risks I took...I was sure I'd die young and nastily. I pictured Cal living to be eighty or ninety. Strange how things work out, isn't it?"

I stare at the hole in the left side of Dervish's chest. Blood is seeping from it and I can see bone inside. "Yeah," I grunt. "Hilarious."

Dervish shifts and grimaces. He's in a lot of pain, but he won't have to suffer much longer. My uncle was in bad shape before we took on an army of demons. Now, having come through hell, he doesn't have a prayer. He's finished. We both know it. That's why we came up here from the underground cave, so he could die in the open, breathing fresh air.

"I remember one time," Dervish continues, "not long after Cal married your mum. We had a huge fight. He wanted me to quit being a Disciple, marry and have kids, lead a normal life. He thought I was crazy to do what I did."

"He wasn't wrong," I snort.

"You love it really," Dervish grins. Blood trickles down his chin.

"Save your breath," I tell him, trying not to shudder.

"What for? I won't need it where I'm going." He raises an eyebrow. "You don't think I can survive, do you?"

"Of course not. I'm just sick of listening to you whine."

Dervish laughs softly. The laugh turns into a blood-drenched cough. I hold him as he shakes and moans, spewing up blood and phlegm. When the fit passes, he asks me to move him out of the cave. "I don't think I need worry about sunburn," he murmurs.

I pick up my dying uncle and carry him outside. He doesn't weigh much. Thin and drawn, overstretched by the world. He rests his head on my chest, like a baby cuddling up to its mother. I prop him against a large rock, then settle beside him. His eyes stay closed. He's dozed off. I study him sadly, memorizing every line of his creased face, brushing the wilting spikes of hair back from his forehead, remembering all the nights he comforted me when I'd had a nightmare.

With a jolt he wakes and looks around, alarmed. When he sees me, and the hole in his chest, he relaxes. "Oh, it was only a dream. I thought we were in trouble."

"Nothing can trouble us here."

Dervish smiles at me lopsidedly. "I loved having you live with me. You were like my son. Billy was too, but I never got to spend the sort of time with him that I did with you."

"If you were my real dad, I'd have asked to be put into foster care."

Dervish's smile widens. "That's what I like to hear. You're a true Grady. We don't do sympathetic."

His eyes wander and he sighs. "I hope I see Cal again. Billy and Meera. Even Beranabus. So many who've gone before me. Do you think there's an afterlife, Grubbs? Will I be reborn? Or is there just... nothing?"

"There has to be *something*," I mutter. "Why would the universe give us souls if not? It'd be pointless."

Dervish nods slowly, then frowns at something behind me. "What's that?" he wheezes.

My head shoots around and I scan the surrounding area for danger. But I can't see anything except dry earth and rocks. "There's nothing—" I begin, then stop. Dervish's eyes have glazed over. He's not breathing. His face is calm.

I tremble and reach out to close his eyelids, blinking back tears. My fingers are just a few inches from his eyes when... *snap!* Dervish's teeth clamp together and he bites the tip of my index finger.

"Hellfire!" I roar, toppling backwards, heart racing.

"Your face," Dervish snickers—always the bloody joker!

"Try it again," I snarl. "Next time I'll dig a hole and bury you alive."

"Don't be so sensitive," Dervish coos, still giggling. He runs an eye over my unnatural muscles, the tufts of red hair sprouting from my skin, my wolfish features, yellow eyes, jagged claws, and blood-spattered fangs. "You're a real mess."

"With a role model like you, I never had a hope," I sniff.

"Poor Grubbs." Dervish makes goo-goo eyes at me. "All you ever wanted was for someone to show you some love."

"Get stuffed."

We both laugh.

"I'm going to miss you," Dervish sighs.

"Yeah," I mutter. "I'll...y'know...you too."

"Part of me wishes I could hang on and see how it all turns out. But then I think about the odds..." He shakes his head.

"Don't worry," I say grandly. "I'll take care of the Demonata. The Shadow too. I've seen enough movies to know how these things end. We'll all be high-fiving each other and celebrating a glorious victory by this time next month. But you won't see any of it. Because you'll be dead."

Dervish scowls. "You really know how to comfort a dying man."

We're silent awhile. The flow of blood has slowed, but I don't kid myself—it's only because he doesn't have much left. There's no getting better, not this time. Dervish has cheated death for the last few months, but he played his last card when we faced the demon hordes.

"What's going to become of you, Grubbs?" he asks. "This new look...the way you kill so freely..."

"I'll be fine." I poke the ground with my bare, hairy toes.

"No," he says. "You've changed, and not just on the outside." He lays a weak, bloodstained hand on mine. "Don't become a monster. Remember who you are, the people who love you, why you fight. Beranabus acted inhumanly, but he was never fully human to begin with. You were. You *are*. Don't lose track of that."

"Is this really how you want to go?" I squint. "Lecturing me like some second-rate TV psychiatrist?"

"I'm serious," he growls.

"Don't be stupid," I smile. "It's far too late for that."

Dervish rolls his eyes, then shrugs. "Don't say I didn't warn you."

"I won't."

Dervish shivers and glares at the sun. "It's so cold. Why's there no warmth in that thing?"

"Eclipse." It's the first thing that pops into my head. Dervish cocks an eyebrow but otherwise ignores the inanity.

"I wish we could have had more leisure time," he says. "Apart from the trip to Slawter, I never took you on any vacations."

"If Slawter was your idea of a vacation, that was probably a good thing."

"Orlando," Dervish nods. "That's where we should have gone. Roller coasters. You, Billy, and me. We'd have had so much fun."

"We were never meant for a life like that," I mumble. "I used to think I could choose it, just turn my back on magic and demons. But I've been locked into this course since birth, just like you. Bec, Beranabus—all of us—we never really had a choice. I hate the unfairness of fate, but..."

I pause. Dervish's head has slumped. I tilt his head back, keeping my fingers clear of his mouth, expecting him to bite again. But this time it isn't a joke. His eyes are closed. The last breath has slipped from his semi-parted lips. His heart has stopped beating.

"Guess the last laugh's on you, old-timer," I croak, letting his head rest on my shoulder and patting him clumsily.

Rising, I gently lay him back against the rock, then pad away and choose a spot in the shade. As I bend, I get the feeling that Dervish is sneaking up on me. I turn quickly, lips lifting into a smile, but he hasn't moved. He never will again.

Sighing emptily, I clench my fingers tightly, then drive them into the dry, hard-packed soil, scooping out the first fistful of my dead uncle's grave.

CLOCKING OFF

✠   ✠   ✠

CREEPING through a factory, in pursuit of a snake demon twenty-five feet long. I wouldn't have thought a beast that size could hide easily, but I've been searching for several minutes without success. I should be out on the streets, battling the masses, but this demon killed a Disciple. She was an elderly, frail lady, but she could swing a spike-headed mace more effectively than anyone I've ever met. I never asked her name, but I liked her. I'm going to make her killer pay.

I slide around a corner, checking the pipes overhead. I feel edgy, which is odd. I haven't felt anything but cold, detached hatred recently. I guess the tension of the moment has got to me. I'm sure the demon won't prove to be a serious threat — I'm more than a match for any of the familiars who cross through windows — but it's fun to pretend I'm in danger. I'd almost forgotten what fear was like.

A scraping noise behind me. I whirl, a ball of magical energy crackling at my fingertips. But it's only Moe. He followed me into the building, even though I told him to stay outside. Moe's one of three werewolves who've been with me since Wolf Island. Werewolves don't need names, but after a few weeks with the trio, I felt like I should call them something. So I christened them Curly, Larry, and Moe, after the Three Stooges. I never had much time for the Stooges, but Dervish loved them, so I named the werewolves in his memory.

I growl at Moe to let him know I'm displeased. He makes a soft whining noise, but he can tell I'm not that bothered. Moe takes his bodyguard duties seriously. He never likes to be too far from me. I think he feels a bit lost when I'm not there for him to protect.

Letting Moe fall into place behind me, I push farther into the factory, past a long conveyor belt. Workers were sitting in the chairs alongside it just an hour ago. It's been nearly a month since Dervish died in the desert. There have been dozens of crossings since then. Hundreds of thousands of humans have been killed. People are terrified and desperate, but life goes on. A few of us know the cause is hopeless, but we haven't shared the bad news. As far as the general population is concerned, we can beat these demonic invaders. So, as the body count mounts, folk carry on normally, manning their posts even in the face of an impending crossing, slipping away to safety at the last moment, returning as soon as the window closes.

Moe growls and darts to a nearby locker. I start to follow, assuming it's the demon, but when he rips the locker door off and tears open a lunchbox, I realize he's found a sandwich.

"Idiot," I grunt, turning back to the conveyor belt.

Fangs sink into my thigh. Yelling, I fall and the snake drags me into the gloom beneath the belt, where it's been lying in wait. I strike at its eyes, but it doesn't have any. Gripping me tightly, it drives its fangs farther into my flesh, crushing the bones in my leg.

I once read a survival pamphlet that said if a giant snake ever got hold of you, you should lie still, so it thinks you are dead. Then, as it swallows your legs, you free your knife (too bad if you don't have one) and hold it by your side. As the snake devours your thighs and sets to work on your stomach, you drive the tip of the knife up through the roof of its mouth and deep into its brain. That always grossed out girls when I told them!

I'm sure it's sound advice, but I don't have time to test it. Unlike most large snakes, this demon's poisonous and I can feel its venom coursing through my veins. I don't have the luxury of playing possum. Besides, that's not my style.

Grunting against the pain, I grab the demon's fangs and snap them off. The beast chokes and releases me, spewing poisonous pink blood. I drive one of the broken fangs into the side of its head. It squeals like a baby and thrashes across the floor. I hang on, riding it bronco-style, stabbing at it again and again. More blood froths from the wounds, soaking my face and chest.

As the snake slams against the conveyor belt, knocking it over, I thrust my head in its mouth and roar down its throat. A ball of magic bursts from my lips and rips through the demon's body. It explodes into tattered, slimy shreds. I pick some of the foul scraps from between my teeth, then focus magic into my leg and repair the damage. Getting to my feet, I look for Moe. He's still munching the sandwich.

"Great help you were," I snarl, using more magic to clear my veins of poison.

Moe looks at me guiltily, then holds out the last piece of sandwich. I turn my nose up at it and hobble for the doorway, eager to squeeze in more killing before the window between universes shuts and robs me of my demonic punching bags.

✠ The streets are awash with demons, the usual assortment of vile concoctions, many cobbled together from bodies resembling those of animals, fish, and birds. Demons are an unimaginative lot. Most can use magic to mold their forms, but rather than give themselves original, amazing bodies, they copy ours.

Dozens of werewolves are fighting the demons. I had them imported from Wolf Island, to replace those of my original pack. Most of the new specimens aren't as sturdy, fast, or smart as those I first chose, but they get the job done. Curly's in the middle of them, acting as pack leader in my absence. She's a fierce creature, taller than me, though not as broad. Sharp too. She can always spot if one of the werewolves disobeys orders and attacks a human instead of a demon. She pounces on the offending party in an instant and slits the beast's throat without blinking. No second chances with Curly.

Soldiers and freshly blooded mages support the werewolves. The soldiers don't do much damage—you can only kill a demon with magic—but the mages are doing a pretty good job. They're learning quickly. Not up to the level of the Disciples, but getting there fast.

I move among the apprentices, taking the place of the mace-wielding old lady. There aren't many Disciples left, so they're spread thinly across the world, one or two per group of mages. I see the men and women around me flinch as I pass. They know who I am. They've seen me kill more demons than anybody else. They know they're safe when I'm around. But I'm a fearsome sight, and most find it hard to suppress a shudder when they find themselves beside me.

I could change back if I wished, resume my human form. But I prefer it this way. It's easier to lead people to their death if you're not truly one of them.

A girl, no more than twelve or thirteen, is playing with a wooden yo-yo. As a demon comes within range, she snaps the yo-yo at it. The wood splinters and the shards puncture the demon's eyes. She replaces it with another yo-yo, this time a plastic one.

"Nice work," I grunt.

She looks up at me and fakes a yawn. "Whatever."

Magic isn't a natural part of our universe. But some humans — mages — are born with the ability to tap into it. When a demon opens a window from its universe to ours, magical energy spills through. If you're a mage, you're in business.

In the past, very few mages got to unleash their power. Windows weren't opened often. It was hard for the Disciples to find new recruits. Now that demons have gone into overdrive, and two or three windows open every day, it's simple.

When a window is forming, we arrange for crowds of people to wait close by, then test them for magical prowess. Those who show promise are thrown into the fray after a quick burst of training, to perish or triumph.

I see a window in the near distance. A child, even younger than the girl with the yo-yo, stands to one side. A man and woman are behind her. I guess they're using the girl. She probably had no choice in this. But, innocent or not, the Demonata are working through her, so she has to die.

As I push through the battling demons, werewolves, and humans, I marvel at the greed of mankind. I should be accustomed to it, but I'm still astonished every time it happens. Most mages use their powers for good, especially now that people can clearly see the full, destructive evil of the Demonata.

But there are others who side with the demons. They seek power, wealth, a longer life. They scent an opportunity to get ahead and sell off their souls to the highest bidder without a second thought. It never seems to occur to them that there will be no place in a demon-run world for *any* humans, even the most evil. Demons don't do coalitions.

The woman behind the girl spots me. She taps the girl's shoulder and mutters in her ear. The three of them edge closer to the window. Uh-uh! Can't have them slipping away early. That wouldn't be fair. I bark a phrase of magic and erect an invisible barrier between the trio and the window. Panic shoots across the faces of the adults. The girl simply looks confused.

The man hurls himself at the barrier, trying to smash it with his shoulder. The woman curses and draws a gun. As she trains it on me, I turn it into a posy of flowers. She stares at the petals, sadness filling her eyes as she realizes this will serve as her death wreath. Then Moe barrels onto the scene and knocks her to the ground. Her screams excite the wolf in me and I fall on the man, snarling. He just has time to beg for mercy. Then my teeth are around his throat and the sweet taste of human flesh fills my mouth.

I gulp the man's blood, then toss his carcass aside and loom over the girl. She gazes up at me, that confused look still crinkling her features. She's even younger than I thought, maybe seven or eight. She's clutching a small teddy bear in one hand.

"Are you the boogey man?" she whispers, eyes round.

"Yes," I croak, then take hold of her head with my huge, scarred, blood-soaked hands and crush.

Thoughts of Juni Swan flicker through my mind as the girl shakes and drops the teddy bear. Juni was Lord Loss's assistant. She could catch glimpses of the future. We fought on Wolf Island. She had me beaten, but then let me go. Because, in a vision, she saw me destroying the world.

I've tried to dismiss Juni's prophecy, but I'm sure it's true. I often think that I should throw myself off a cliff or let the demons kill me. The world would be a safer place without me. But I can't do it. Life's too sweet. So I lie to myself and cling to false hope that she was wrong, even though I know it's selfish madness.

As the girl goes still, I set her down and wonder if I'll crush the world as easily as her head.

The window flashes out of existence, stranding the demons. With screams of despair, they battle furiously, eager to kill as many humans as they can before this universe rids itself of their ugly stain. But they're already weakening, robbed of the magic they need to survive.

I feel my strength fading too. I'm a magician, so I can operate in the absence of a window. But I'm nowhere near as powerful as I am when the air's thick with the delirious energy of the Demonata.

It doesn't matter. I'm not essential in this final stage. Nor are the mages. This is where the werewolves and soldiers come into their own. They rip apart the weakened demons with fangs, claws, bullets, and machetes. The demons don't die, but they no longer have the power to put themselves back together, so they can only lie there in pieces and wait to dissolve as magic drains from the air.

Moe cocks a deformed eyebrow at me and grunts questioningly.

"Go on," I sigh, wincing at the pain in my leg. That's the downside of using magic to heal a wound. It's fine while there's magical energy in the air, but once that passes, pain kicks in with a vengeance.

As Moe joins the bloodletting, a pale, thin, icy-looking woman approaches me. It's Prae Athim, head of the Lambs, a group that once acted as executioners of Grady children who'd turned into werewolves. Now they supply me with fresh recruits from Wolf Island.

"That looks nasty," Prae says, nodding at my leg. It's purple, and pus seeps from the cuts that have reopened.

"I'll be fine," I mutter. "I got rid of all the poison before the window closed."

"Does it hurt?" she asks.

"Yes. But it won't kill me."

"Still, you should have it looked at."

I grin. Prae loves to mother her wolfen wards, even a semi-werewolf like me. She's cold with humans but has a soft spot for those who've turned into savage, mindless killing machines.

"Will you look after the others?" I ask.

"Of course," she snaps. "Don't I always?"

Prae can't directly control the werewolves—only I can do that—but she's had years of experience and commands a team of specialists. When I'm tired or don't have the time to round up the pack and settle them down, she moves in with her troops. They use electric prods, nets, and shackles where necessary, though having feasted on so many demons, most of the werewolves are happy to do as ordered.

"Will I see you later?" I ask. After a battle, Prae often spends the night with me, looking ahead to the next assault, discussing tactics.

"No," she says. "We're accepting a new shipment from the island. I want to make sure the transfer goes smoothly and get them quartered close to the others."

"Do you want my help?"

She shakes her head. "I'll make them comfortable first. You can give them your pep talk in the morning. I'm sure they'll be impressed."

Prae leaves and I chuckle softly. I've grown fond of her in recent weeks. She reminds me of Dervish. He could be a distant customer too, when he needed to be.

Thinking of my dead uncle wipes the smile from my lips. I spend a few minutes remembering some of his finer moments—when he came to see me in the asylum after my family was killed, fighting Vein and Artery in the cellar at Carcery Vale, battling Lord Loss in the town of Slawter, dying with dignity in the desert.

Then I recall his love for Juni, when we thought she was on our side, and that reminds me of her dire prophecy. Sighing miserably, I shuffle off to the hospital, wishing I could avoid quiet, human moments like these. Life's a lot easier when chaos is erupting all around and the beastly wolf within me rises to the fore.

MR. GRUMPY-PUSS

✦   ✦   ✦

I'M not going to the hospital to have myself tended to. Prae's concern was touching but unwarranted. I'll be in a lot of pain until the next attack, but as soon as a window opens and magic floods the air, I'll revive spectacularly. No, I'm going to look in on a patient. A guy not much older than me, whose eyes I clawed out a month ago.

As I enter the ward where I left Kernel before the battle started, I fill with guilt, as I do every time I face him. My stomach still gives a turn when I recall the callous way I blinded my friend, ripping his eyes from their sockets the way a bully might swipe a bag of sweets from a child.

The doctors and nurses are rushed off their feet trying to deal with a flood of wounded. Abandoning the more seriously injured to chance, they focus on those most likely to respond to treatment.

Nobody pays much attention to me as I pad through the corridors. I've made myself a bit smaller, but I still cut a sinister sight. I'm taller and broader than any human, naked except for a pair of torn, tattered pants, hairy, bloody, and foul-smelling. I'd inspire terror if these were normal times. But we've passed way beyond the bounds of normality. These days, in the cities and towns where the war takes me, I draw nothing more than curious glances.

I stop at the door of Kernel's room and study the bald, brown-skinned teenager through the glass. He's sitting on a chair in the corner. I left him lying on a bed, but he's given that up to one of the recently wounded. Kirilli Kovacs is by his side, chatting animatedly, making sweeping gestures with his hands. I smile at the ridiculous Kirilli. He still wears a stage magician's costume, though he replaced his ruined original suit with a new one a few weeks back. It didn't have gold and silver stars down the sides, but he found some and has been stitching them on in quieter moments.

Two fingers on Kirilli's left hand are missing, he's scarred and bruised all over, and his right foot was bitten off at the ankle — he wears a prosthetic. Kirilli is proud of his injuries. He whined to begin with, but when he saw the impression they made on people — especially pretty nurses — he adopted a stoic stance. He loves telling exaggerated tales about how he lost his various body parts.

Kirilli's a natural coward, but he came good when we last fought the demons in their own universe. He was a hero that day, surprising even himself. He hasn't been called into action too often since, but has handled himself capably when required. I think he's over the worst of his cowardice, though he'll never be an out-and-out warrior.

I push the door open. Kernel is smiling at whatever tall tale Kirilli's spinning. The pair have become good friends.

Kirilli helps Kernel forget about his missing eyes. I should really set the Disciple more demanding tasks—he's too important to waste on babysitting duties—but guilt over what I did to Kernel stays my hand.

There's a growl to my left. It's Larry, crouched in the corner. I leave one of my most trusted werewolves with Kernel whenever I'm not around. Officially they're here to protect him. But the truth—as Kernel knows—is that I don't trust my blind companion. I'm afraid he'll create a pair of eyes when a window is open and slip away. Larry's instructions—hammered into him with difficulty—are to watch over Kernel and disable him if the teenager ever starts fiddling with his sockets.

Kernel and Kirilli glance up when Larry growls. Kernel's expression instantly changes, even though he can't see me. I guess the smell gives me away.

"Here comes our triumphant general," Kernel sneers. "Kill many demons today, Grubbs? *Blind* any of them?"

"How is he?" I ask Kirilli, ignoring the taunts.

"Blind!" Kernel snaps before the Disciple can answer. "In agony. A doctor had a look at me earlier, before the window opened. Infection has set in. I used magic to clean it—carefully, so as not to arouse my *guard's* suspicions—but the rot will return. I'll probably drop dead of some disease of the brain any day now. Give me back my eyes, you son of a wolfen hound!"

"Does he ever change the track?" I sigh.

"He only gets like this when you're around," Kirilli murmurs. "And, as I'm sure you acknowledge, he has genuine cause for complaint."

I grunt sourly and step aside as a patient is bundled past by a couple of nurses. "We've had this conversation too many times. I won't restore your eyes until we rescue Bec. If you promised not to take off, I'd let you fix them now."

"I promise to kick your ass every day for all eternity in hell," Kernel snarls. "How about that?"

I scowl at the blind magician, hating myself more than him. Kernel's part of a demonic weapon known as the Kah-Gash. I am too. It can be used to settle this war, handing ultimate victory to us or the Demonata. The third part is in a girl called Bec, currently a prisoner of the demon master, Lord Loss.

The original plan was for the three of us to unite, unleash the power of the Kah-Gash, destroy the Demonata, and ride off into the sunset, champions of the universe, the greatest heroes ever. Easy.

Then Death came along and complicated matters. Death used to be a force, the same as gravity or light, without thought or form. Now it has a mind and it created a body from the souls of the dead that it reaped. We christened it the Shadow before we found out its true identity.

Death doesn't like us. Life's too abundant in this universe. It wants to go back to the way things were, when only demons and the Old Creatures were around. It's thrown its support behind the Demonata. Under Death's guidance, the demons have banded together and launched an assault on Earth. Their reward if they triumph will be the obliteration of mankind, control of our universe, and immortality. Not a bad little package!

One of the ancient Old Creatures took Kernel on a trip

to the center of the universe, explaining the origins of life along the way. Apparently there was one universe to begin with, divided into sixty-four zones, half white and half black, like a chessboard. The Kah-Gash held it all together, keeping the demons and Old Creatures apart. Then law and order broke down, the Big Bang shattered everything, and life as we know it began.

The Old Creatures protected us from the Demonata as long as they could, but they've been fighting a losing battle. Unlike the demons, they can't reproduce, so when the last one dies, we'll be left to the devices of the inhuman armies. That spells curtains for this world and all the others in our universe.

To deny the demons their triumph, the Old Creatures created an ark. Like Noah's, only this is an entire world, staffed by a variety of the universe's more magical creatures. They want Kernel to captain the ark. As the *eyes* of the Kah-Gash, he can find shortcuts between any two points in the universe. By keeping him alive forever, the Old Creatures hope that he can steer the ark one step ahead of the pursuing Demonata, ensuring that a small section of our universe survives until the end of time.

It would have been easy for Kernel to accept their offer. But he came back and pitched in with us for one last assault. The Old Creatures said we couldn't beat Death, that it's invulnerable, but Kernel refused to write off our chances. He joined with Bec and me, and we confronted the Shadow.

We managed to destroy Death's body, but it's only a matter of time before it returns, bigger and badder than before, to lead its followers to victory. Seeing this, Kernel chose to return to the ark. I asked him to stay and fight. Bec had been captured by Lord Loss and I wanted us to free her, then unleash the full force of the Kah-Gash on Death when it returned.

Kernel refused. He thought Bec had switched allegiances and sided with Lord Loss. Even if she hadn't, he couldn't see any way of defeating Death. He got ready to open a window and take off for pastures unimaginably distant.

That's when I lost my cool and tore out his eyes. I needed Kernel to find Bec for us to stand any sort of chance against Death. If I had to blind and imprison him to force his hand, so be it. The human Grubbs Grady could never have acted so viciously, but the new, wolfen me... Well, I don't sleep with an easy conscience, but I can live with it.

"How does he look?" Kernel asks Kirilli. "Ashamed? He should. What he did to me, I wouldn't have done to a dog. Or a demon. Not even a werewolf."

"He looks tired," Kirilli says, offering me a slight smile.

"Poor Grubbs," Kernel sneers. "Are you overworked? You should take a week off, treat yourself to a vacation."

"That's right," I sigh. "Go on hating me. It's not like you've got anything else to hate, is it?"

"The Demonata?" Kernel shakes his head. "I *don't* hate them. They're doing what they were born to. Nature spat them out as foul, heartless killers. That's the way they are. You, on the other hand, chose vileness over humanity. We were friends. I trusted you. But then you did this to me and keep me here against my will, even though you know it's wrong. I despise you more than I ever thought possible."

I sniff away his insults. "Whatever," I deadpan, echoing the girl with the yo-yo. "We're staying here the rest of the night, then moving out at ten in the morning. If you want anything, ask a nurse."

"I want new eyes," Kernel snarls. "Can a nurse fetch me those?"

I start for the door.

"Grubbs," Kernel stops me. I glance back wearily, preparing myself for more insults. "Why are we still here?"

I frown. "I told you, we're staying overnight, then—"

"I mean on Earth," he interrupts. "When you blinded me, you said you needed me to find Bec, that we'd wait for our wounds to heal, then rescue her. But it's been a month and we haven't gone after her. Why not?"

I'm surprised Kernel hasn't mentioned this before. I kept waiting for him to ask and had all sorts of responses lined up. But now my tongue freezes. I flash on the dreams I've been having, think about sharing them with him, then shake my head.

"We're not ready. We'll go for Bec when the time is right. We can do more good here at the moment."

"*We?*" Kernel replies archly. "All I do is wait around in hospitals for you to return from the killing fields. If you're not going to use me, set me free."

"I will use you," I mutter. "When it's time, I'll take you back to the demon universe and let you build new eyes."

"And then?" Kernel prompts.

"We'll find Bec."

"*Find* her?" He pounces like a cat. "Not *rescue* her?"

I gulp, then nod at Kirilli. "I'll see you in the morning."

"Not if I see you first," Kernel calls after me, then raises his voice as I exit, to make sure I hear his parting shot. "Not that *that's* very likely!"

✠ I find an unoccupied room on an upper floor of the hospital and make a bed out of some balled-up surgical gowns. I'd rather not sleep, but rest is vital, even for a creature like me. I have to be at my sharpest to keep on fighting demons.

I think about my conversation with Kernel, and about Dervish, Juni, Lord Loss, Bec. I recall the prophecy again, the way Juni cackled, her delight as she described seeing the world explode, the universe burning beneath my twisted hands.

It's too much. Guilt, fear, and loneliness overwhelm me. I'm not in close touch with my human emotions these days. I've become a detached, brutal excuse for a person. But tonight, for a few brief minutes, my defenses crumble. I become an awkward teenager again. I feel the weight of the expectations that ride upon me...the awful price the world will pay if I fail...those who've been lost...the lives I've taken, like the confused little girl tonight...the fear of what might be waiting for me when I cross to Lord Loss's realm...Juni's prophecy.

As my face contorts and becomes more human, my chest heaves and I weep. Hot, thick, salty tears run down my cheeks as I sob and beg for help from the dead—Dervish and Beranabus, Mum and Dad, Meera and Bill-E. I've blinded a friend. Hidden terrible truths from those who've placed their trust in me. Killed and lied. And, if Juni's to be believed, there's worse to come.

I wail and mumble madly, biting into the gowns to stifle my cries, pounding my chest and face with my fists. I curse the universe, God if he exists, the Old Creatures, the Disciples, Lord Loss, and all the demons. But most of all I curse myself, poor, pitiful, apocalyptic Grubbs Grady.

Then, as the tears dry...as the werewolf regains control and my features harden and transform...as I bury my humanity deep again...as the Kah-Gash whispers and tells me I'm not alone and to stop behaving like a child...I gradually calm down.

I turn and readjust the gowns. Make myself comfortable. Breathe more slowly. Mutter a short spell. And fall into what should be a pure and dreamless sleep—but isn't.

IN DREAMS I WALK
WITH YOU

�֍   ✦   ✦

THE spell I use when I want to sleep is supposed to stop me dreaming. It's designed to provide me with a good night's sleep, free of nightmares, so I can wake fresh and bright in the morning. But it hasn't been working since Bec was abducted. I've tried different spells, having asked a number of Disciples for advice, but nothing keeps the dream at bay. The same disturbing scenes unfold every time, and they're the real reason why I haven't tried to rescue Bec.

As the dream kicks in again, I flow along with it as usual. I've tried fighting, struggled to change the sequence or details, but without success. Tonight I accept my lack of control with as much grace as a savage beast like me can muster.

I'm in a room made of cobwebs, staring down at a sleeping girl — Bec. She lies on a bed of thick webs, covered by a blanket of much finer strands. She looks pale and exhausted but bears no wounds and breathes easily, calmly.

Her left hand moves upwards and brushes her cheek,

as I knew it would. Her nose twitches and again I'm not surprised. I've seen it all a dozen times. When you experience the same dream over and over, you start paying attention to the details, to stop yourself going mad. I try to find something new tonight, a little movement or quiver that I missed before, but everything is exactly the same.

Bec's eyelids flutter open. A moment of panic—"Where am I?"—then her look of alarm fades and she rises. She's dressed in a beautiful nightgown, the sort I've only seen in old movies. It's not made of webs. I guess Lord Loss took it from one of his victims—I can't imagine him going shopping for it.

Bec walks to a small, round window and gazes out over a landscape of cobwebs. This is Lord Loss's realm, a world of countless sticky strands, a massive network of despair and sorrow. The air is thick with misery and suffering. I can sense that thousands of people have died here, crying out for their loved ones, alone and separated from all they'd ever known.

Bec turns to a table and chair, both carved out of webs. There's a mirror set in the wall over the table. The girl sits and studies her reflection. She looks tense but not scared. She reaches out to touch the face in the mirror, as if she's not sure it's really hers, then pauses and lowers her hand.

Standing, she walks to a wardrobe on the other side of the room. The doors open as she approaches, and a clothes rack slides out. Long, frilly dresses hang from it, the sort a princess or movie star would wear. I don't think they'd suit a plain girl like Bec. She must think the same thing because she smiles at the dresses and shakes her head.

"You do yourself a disservice, Little One," says a voice. Bec stiffens, then turns slowly and regards Lord Loss. He's hovering in the doorway, blood seeping from the many cracks in his pale red skin. His dark red eyes are as kindly as I've ever seen them. Even the snakes in the hole where his heart should be look harmless, hissing playfully, seeming to smile at the young girl by the wardrobe.

"Of course you deserve such finery," Lord Loss continues, floating into the room and running a couple of his eight arms over the dresses. "You are a priestess of high standing. You should expect only the best from your world and its people. They exist to serve your pleasure and revere your beauty."

"You flatter me," Bec says shyly.

"No," Lord Loss says. "Power is beauty, and as you are the most powerful of all humans, you must be the most beautiful. Wear these dresses and think of them as rags. We shall find finer robes for you later."

He picks out a green dress and smiles. "This matches your eyes. Will you try it on, to please me?"

"Very well." Bec sighs and slips out of her nightdress, not embarrassed to be naked in front of the demon master. Bec's nudity made me uncomfortable at first, but I'm used to it now. What I find more unsettling is the fact that she seems to want to please Lord Loss. Why should she care about his wishes, or dress to impress him? This is our enemy, a vile, twisted monster. Yet she's letting him treat her like a doll.

When Bec has dressed, Lord Loss leads her to the table and applies makeup as she sits patiently. It's obscene, watching his mangled hands brushing across her face. I want to knock him away and slap Bec back to her senses. It wouldn't be so bad if he was controlling her thoughts, brainwashing her to do his bidding. But I don't get any hint of that. Bec looks nervous, but her mind appears to be her own.

When Lord Loss is finished, he drifts back a few feet and studies her. He nods with satisfaction, as he does every time, and murmurs, "What a vision."

Bec blushes, unable to hide a timid smile. I've grown to loathe that smile. It's wrong. This should be a place of tears and heartache, not shy smirks.

"Come," Lord Loss says, offering Bec an arm. "Let me show you more of my palace."

Bec gulps, then takes his arm and lets the demon master lead her out of the bedroom. They descend a staircase of webs. Some of Lord Loss's familiars scurry past as the pair walk gracefully down the steps. The lesser demons scowl at Bec but steer clear of her, afraid of angering their master. Bec knows they hate her, but she doesn't care. She's safe as long as she stays by her protector.

They stroll through the castle, Lord Loss polite as a prince, the perfect host, pointing out features of special interest. Bec admires the chandeliers and statues, and coos when Lord Loss modestly admits to designing them himself.

"You're so creative," she says.

"That is kind of you, but untrue," he replies. "They're modeled after objects I have seen on Earth. I have a certain workmanlike skill but no real artistic streak. Unoriginality is the curse of my kind."

They descend farther, to a cellar deep beneath the

ground. In my sleep I tense. I know what's coming and I hate it. This is one of the worst parts of the dream. If I could skip it, I would, but it draws me on as it always does, an unwilling viewer, unable to pull back or look aside.

We enter a chamber of torture. Savage implements of torment are strapped to the webby walls. Brands glow red in burning fires. The air is pierced by the screams of the dying. Bec flinches and her fingers tighten on Lord Loss's arm. He pats her small hand, comforting her. She gulps, then takes a trembling step forward. Lord Loss nods approvingly and leads her on.

I've never been able to count all the people in the cellar, since many are hidden behind walls or cabinets. There are at least thirty, probably a lot more, to judge by the volume of shrieks and moans.

"Do you feel sorry for them?" Lord Loss asks as Bec shudders.

"Yes," she whimpers.

"Good," he says. "Pity is a virtue. I feel sorry for them too. It's true," he insists as she shoots him a dubious glance. "I take pleasure from their torment, but I feel pity too. That is how I differ from my fellow demons. I don't hate humanity. I crave their torment and sorrow, but I also adore them. I torture with love, Little One. Can you understand that?"

"No," she frowns.

He sighs. "At least you are honest. I'm glad you can reveal your true feelings to me. I don't want there to be any deception between us. Always tell me the truth, even if you think I won't like it. Lies belittle us all."

Bec observes silently as Lord Loss sets to work on a few

of the humans hanging from the walls or lying across hard tables. He acts like a nurse as he tortures them, every movement deceptively gentle and loving. He purrs softly, telling them how sorry he is, how he wishes he could free them, how it won't be much longer now.

Bec doesn't look as if she shares the demon master's enjoyment, but she doesn't object either. I've tried to read her mind every time we get to this point, but I can't. I'd give anything to know what's in her thoughts. I hope she's putting on a detached face to fool Lord Loss, to stay on his good side and trick him into thinking she doesn't hate him. I hope this is a masterful act, that she's plotting to betray him, waiting and praying for Kernel and me to burst in and rescue her.

But her eyes are calm and emotionless, and when she licks her lips, it looks as if she's fighting a desire to try what Lord Loss is doing.

As the demon master continues to extract fresh pain from his victims, Bec casts her gaze around, and my virtual head swivels too. This is the part I hate the most. I try to look away or shut my eyes, but I'm locked in. I have to see what she sees, even though it sends a chill through my bones that will still be there when I wake.

The people chained to the walls and torture devices are a varied mix. Men and women, boys and girls, of different races. No babies — Lord Loss likes to be able to hold discussions with his victims. With a single exception, I don't recognize any of them, though I know by his magical aura that one — a thin, blond-haired man — is a Disciple.

Bec studies the Disciple — he's in the worst shape of all,

kept alive only by magic—then moves on, her gaze sweeping over a girl my age. I didn't notice her the first few times. To Bec she's of no more interest than any of the others. It's a blink-and-you-miss-it moment. It was only after the fourth or fifth time, when I was concentrating on details to keep boredom at bay, that I focused on the girl's face and got a shock that echoes even now, twenty or so viewings later.

The girl is pretty, but her face is covered with blood and scrunched up with terror. Her clothes hang from her in filthy rags, but I'm sure they originally came from the finest designer boutiques. And although her hair is a tangled mess and her nails are long and cracked, once they were as carefully tended as a model's.

Apart from the blood, the girl doesn't seem to have been tortured, but many of Lord Loss's victims look unmarked. He patches them up and lets them recover a little when he's done, to make it all the more painful next time. Inside, I'm sure she's been twisted and torn in more ways than most humans could imagine.

As Bec's eyes dart about, I snatch the same quick glimpse of the girl that I've been horrified by ever since I realized who she was. Back on Earth, in a quiet hospital room, my lips move as I mutter in my sleep. *"Bo Kooniart…"*

EXECUTIVE BOARD

✠　　✠　　✠

BEC and Lord Loss move on eventually, up another set of stairs, to a different part of the demon master's palace. Blood drips from his doughy flesh as he floats along, but it's not his own. Bec is silent, head bowed, brooding.

I'm thinking about Bo Kooniart. It seems like a lifetime since I last saw her, racing back into a demon-infested town in search of her horrible father and pain of a brother. Bo was one of the actresses in *Slawter*, a movie about demons made by a crazed director who decided to use real-life monsters in the name of art.

I despised Bo. Her father, Tump Kooniart, was a powerful agent, which was the only reason she and her brother were cast in the film. He was working in league with the director and Lord Loss. He thought the Demonata would spare him and his children. He thought wrong.

Bo was a spoiled, snobbish, sneering little brat. But when the demons ran riot and our lives hung in the balance, she acted selflessly, heroically. We might not have escaped without her help. Then, rather than follow us to freedom, she went back to try to rescue her father and brother.

I assumed Bo had been killed along with the hundreds of others who died, but Lord Loss must have spared her and taken her to his own universe, where he could torture her at his leisure.

When I realized Bo was still alive, trapped in that chamber of nightmares, I felt that I was directly to blame. Lord Loss authorized the attack on the film set in order to wreak revenge on Dervish and me. All those people died because of us. Bo is in torment because of *me.* I feel compelled to cross and break her out. But I don't dare, not until I've decided what to do about Bec. I might get away with one sneak attack on Lord Loss's kingdom, but never two.

The tour continues. Bec is quiet for the most part and looks gloomy, but I'm sure I'd look a lot worse in her position. How can she walk alongside that beast so calmly? Unless she's considering joining him...

I wish they'd have a conversation about it. In movies, the villain always gives his plan away by talking too much and revealing his secrets. But Lord Loss never discusses Bec's state of mind. There's no mention of the war between the Demonata and mankind, or what role he wants Bec to play in it.

The pair enter a room filled with chessboards, and the demon master's face lights up. After our showdown in Slawter, he said I'd spoiled chess for him, but that's not true. He's still a fanatic, as evidenced by the care he takes of the boards and the way he describes them to Bec, telling her where he got them, the games he's played, the opponents he's faced.

"Did you carve any of these yourself?" Bec asks.

"No," he says morosely. "I started to, several times, but chess is like a religion for me. Whenever I sat down to make a set of my own, it felt like sacrilege."

Bec looks around at the array. She seems to be searching for one in particular. "What about the original Board?" she asks eventually.

"Why do you seek that?" Lord Loss's eyes narrow.

"I don't *seek* it," Bec smiles. "I'd just like to see it again. I know you took it from the cave after Drust died."

"You mean after you killed him," Lord Loss murmurs.

Bec stiffens, then tilts her head. "Aye."

Lord Loss clicks several fingers. A demon with five legs and a neck like a giraffe scurries away and returns with a crystal board, the first that was ever made on this world. According to Kernel, it was a tool of the Old Creatures. They used it to help mankind evolve.

Lord Loss holds the Board reverently, then passes it to Bec. She treats it the same careful way he did, examining it closely. "It's amazing," she whispers. "I can feel the power, so different from ours."

"The magic of the Old Creatures," Lord Loss sniffs. "It's nothing special."

Bec hides a smirk behind the Board. I don't see what all the fuss is about. It's just another chessboard as far as I'm concerned. I know it has magical properties, but I've seen a hundred more fascinating objects in my travels.

Bec hands the Board back to Lord Loss. The dream's almost over. I'm anticipating the end. But before the conclusion, there will be one last conversation.

"I'd like to enter it," Bec says.

"Why?" Lord Loss snaps suspiciously.

"I know of its splendors. Kernel went there once, many years ago. I want to experience them for myself."

Lord Loss is frowning. "You cannot escape me in there," he growls. "If you think you can tap into the magic of the Old Creatures and use it against me, you are gravely mistaken."

"That's not my intention," Bec says calmly. "You said earlier that you didn't want me to lie. So I'll tell you truthfully, I *do* have a secret reason for wanting to enter the Board. But it has nothing to do with escape."

Bec's eyes flicker. It's the furtive look of someone who suspects she is being watched, who wants to go somewhere private to discuss dark deeds. I think, as I've thought every time I see her eyes move, Does she know I'm here?

This is no normal dream. I'm certain these events are real, that they happened, are happening, or will happen in the future. I suspect my ability to follow Bec through the castle is the work of the Kah-Gash. If I'm correct, maybe it's working through her too, and she can sense me watching.

Maybe Lord Loss senses Bec's nervousness too, because after a brief pause, he accepts her request. "Very well. I will grant your wish, as I grant the wishes of all who are honest with me."

The pair go rigid and their eyes frost over. Their souls have entered the Board. If I knew for sure that this was happening in the present, I'd cross immediately and strike while the demon master's soul was absent. I'd kill him where he stood, and that would be the end of lowly Lord Loss.

But time works differently in the demon universe. This might be something that took place in the past, or that hasn't happened yet. I'd be a fool if I rushed in without knowing for certain that the demon master was distracted and defenseless.

I wait for the scene to fade and the dream to pass. It always does at this point. I'll slip into unconsciousness and won't stir until morning. A few more seconds and...

Nothing happens. For several minutes I watch the motionless pair, Lord Loss cradling the Board, Bec leaning close to him, both with their eyes half-closed. I wonder if the scene has frozen, like when a DVD sticks, but then a demon slinks by and I realize time *is* passing.

For the first time ever, the dream is different. I don't know if that's a good or a bad sign. I try looking away from the Board, but my gaze is fixed. I start to fidget, wondering if this is a trap, if my mind will remain stuck here while my body shrivels up and dies. Have I been lured in and ensnared? If so, I can't see any way out. I'm helpless in this dream zone.

Time drags on. Hard to tell how long. I wish I had a watch. I become more certain that I've walked into a trap, that I'm going to perish slowly and stupidly. Then, as I'm cursing myself for being so gullible...

Bec blinks, and Lord Loss clutches the Board to his chest. The pair breathe out and smile shakily at each other. "Interesting," Lord Loss mutters.

"Isn't it?" Bec grins.

"I will need time to ponder and reflect."

"Of course."

"If you're wrong...if it doesn't go the way you think..." His face darkens.

"It's a risk no matter which way you play it." Bec shrugs, then turns. "I can find my own way back."

She walks out of the room and I automatically trail her, thinking to myself, What the hell? Lord Loss stays where he is, fondling the Board, staring after Bec with an unreadable expression.

✠ I stay with Bec as she weaves through rooms and corridors of webs, eventually ending up back in the bedroom where she started. She looks exhausted. I think more time passed for them inside the Board than it did for me as an onlooker. But what did they do in there? What did they talk about? It sounded like Bec made some sort of an offer to Lord Loss. But *what*?

She undresses and wipes the makeup from her face. Steps into her nightgown, then returns to the seat by the table and stares into the mirror. She looks doubtful, like she's gambled everything and doesn't know which way the dice will roll. For a moment I believe she's tried to persuade Lord Loss to throw in his lot with us. Perhaps she's been playing him all along, waiting until the time was right to sign him up for our side. I have crazy thoughts of the demon master doing a Darth Vader and joining our side to stop the evil Emperor of Death.

But this isn't *Star Wars*, and almost as soon as the childish hope forms, reality knocks a thousand holes in it.

"I reached my conclusion sooner than I anticipated."

Bec turns. Lord Loss has entered the bedroom. He's

smiling. She stands and walks over to him, trembling. "You've decided?"

"Yes." He leans down and kisses her. For a second I think he means to draw the life from her lips, but this is a kiss of passion, not destruction.

"I admire your daring and cunning," he murmurs. "We will proceed as you suggested. If you can find the lode-stones, I'll help open the tunnels."

Bec throws her arms around Lord Loss and hugs him. As she does, I'm torn from my dream. Snapping awake, I hurl myself from my makeshift bed in the hospital, smash a fist into the wall, then howl at the ceiling like a madman.

HOME SWEET HOME

✼   ✼   ✼

I cancel my plans to travel to the city where the next crossing is due. Instead I send the werewolves, under the guidance of Prae Athim and her Lambs. They'll have to handle
this one without me.

I catch a separate plane, with Kernel, Kirilli, Moe, and
Curly. I leave Larry with the other werewolves to keep
them in line. I'm twitching with nerves, unable to forget the
dream for an instant, wondering about the pact Bec made
with Lord Loss, recalling the way she embraced him. The
memory chews me up inside. I wish I'd gone after her as
soon as she was kidnapped, and killed that damn priestess
from the past.

On the plane, I tell Kernel and Kirilli about the dream.
It's essential they know about the threat, in case anything
happens to me.

Kernel hits the roof. "Why didn't you tell us before?" he
roars. I claim innocence—until last night, there was no hint
that Bec might betray us—but he doesn't buy that. "You

should have told us anyw   ...   ...an to hide
something this important."

There's nothing I can say to ...   ...he's
right.

Moe and Curly hate planes. They ...
as far from the windows as they can squir...
noise of the engines and every bump caused by ...
All of the werewolves hate flying. They suffer it only be... ...
they know there will be rich pickings at the other end.

At least we don't have to bother with connecting flights.
The governments and armies of the world work hand-in-
hand with the Disciples now. A jet is put at my disposal as
soon as I ask for one. It makes getting around a hell of a lot
easier.

Kernel is still griping as we hit the runway, saying he
warned me about Bec, that this wouldn't be happening if I'd
listened and that I should return him to the demon universe
and set him free. He insists we're wasting our time trying
to thwart the plans of Bec and Lord Loss. Although many
of the world's lodestones—reservoirs of ancient, magical
power—were destroyed or drained long ago, an unknown
number still exist.

"The locations of most are a mystery to us," Kernel says,
"but Beranabus knew about a few stones that he either
wasn't able to destroy or wanted to keep intact. He never
told us where they were, but Bec absorbs the memories
of everyone she touches, and she spent a lot of time with
Beranabus. She'll lead Lord Loss to the lodestones, and we
can't stop her. We're done for."

Again, I can't argue. The more potent lodestones can

be used to open a tunnel between the demon universe and ours. The Demonata can cross without limits through such tunnels and stay here as long as they remain open, which could be years or even longer—some can stay open until the end of time itself. If Bec and Lord Loss get hold of those stones, this war is finished.

But we have to *try* to stop them. I despise Kernel's defeatist attitude. And we're not entirely helpless—if Kernel's eyes are restored, he can target Bec and we can maybe kill her before they get going. But I don't say that to him because it would set him off on another rant.

A helicopter is waiting for us when we disembark—again, a perk of the job. I've never ridden in a helicopter for fun. I'm always zipping off to one fight or another. I'd like to take a scenic flight one day, but the way things are stacking up against us, I doubt that will ever happen.

Once we're all strapped in, we take off. Curly and Moe howl happily and stick their heads out of the windows. As much as they hate planes, they love helicopters. Werewolves—go figure!

It's a short flight, and although Kernel carries on with his tirade, I tune him out, thinking about the past, my history, all that I've lost and left behind. I haven't been back here since the night Bill-E died—the night I killed him. Scores of dark memories bob to the surface, mixed in with happier recollections.

We hit the outskirts of Carcery Vale and skim over the houses, shops, and schools. They look unfamiliar from up high. It's evening and the streets are quiet, with only a few people strolling or driving around. We might be facing the end of the world, but life carries on as normal for the most part.

The plan was to head straight to the cave, but on an impulse I lean forward, tap the pilot's shoulder, and point him in a different direction.

"What are you doing?" Kernel asks, feeling the helicopter bank around.

"I want to visit the mansion first."

"What's the point? If we're going to do this, let's crack on and do it. We don't have time for trips down memory lane."

I ignore him and watch intently as we home in on the massive house a few miles outside the town. This is where I lived with Dervish after my parents were slaughtered. It's the last place I was able to call home. Probably the last place I'll *ever* be able to call home.

We touch down in the large courtyard, and the pilot kills the engines. Curly and Moe are first out, sniffing the ground, marking their territory, making sure it's safe for their leader. I slide out next, leaving Kirilli to help Kernel down. The pilot stays with the helicopter.

I stare up at the gigantic house, recalling a variety of memories, a mix of good and bad. The glass in the windows has been shattered by gunfire, but otherwise the building looks much the way it did when I cast my final look back on that sad night.

The spare key isn't under the pot to the left of the front doors, and I prepare to break in. But when I try the doors, they're not locked. Entering, I call "Hello?" but nobody answers. There are no noises apart from the creakings of the house.

As the others follow me in, I spot scores of bullet holes in the walls and ornate old staircase that is the spine of the house, and much of the furniture has been torn to pieces. On Dervish and Bec's last night here, they were attacked by soldiers in the employ of Antoine Horwitzer, a rogue Lamb.

"It smells stale," Kirilli says, limping along behind me.

"It's been deserted for ages," I tell him.

"Not that long," Kernel mutters.

"Perhaps it's mourning the death of its owner," Kirilli says. "Houses have feelings too. They don't live and feel like we do, but they absorb part of the spirit of those who inhabit them."

"Weirdo," Kernel grunts, and I laugh with him. Kirilli shrugs and shuffles off to explore.

"Do you want to come with me?" I ask Kernel, feeling faint traces of the bond that once existed between us.

"No," he sighs, moving to a window and standing by it as if he can see out. "I'll stay here and admire the moonlight. You go cheer up the house. Grubbs?" he adds softly as I turn to pad up the stairs. "I know how much this place means to you. Take your time."

"Thanks." I smile.

I head for Dervish's office first. This is the room he spent most of his time in, where he worked, plotted, and relaxed. It's been shot up badly, but it still reeks of my uncle. His books lie scattered across the floor. His computers have been blown to smithereens, but I can picture him hunched over the screens, frowning as he read about some old spell or other. And maybe it's just my imagination, but I'm sure I can smell the musty stench of his feet—he loved to kick off his shoes in here, but he wasn't great at changing his socks regularly.

I want to say something to mark the occasion and pay homage to the memory of my dead uncle. But everything I think of seems trite and clichéd. I was never the best with words. They've failed me often in the past, and they fail me again now. In the end I just pat the back of the chair where Dervish used to sit.

I visit the hall of portraits and run my gaze over the faces of the dead, all our family members who have perished over the centuries, most as a result of lycanthropy. I'd like to add photos of Dervish and Bill-E to the rows of frames, but I don't have any on me. I could fetch a couple from the study, but I don't want to go back there.

I settle for writing their names in the dusty glass of a couple of the larger pictures, along with their dates of birth and death. Pausing, I smile and add a line under Dervish's name. "Died fighting the good fight." A longer pause, then, with no smile, I write under Bill-E's name, "Killed by his half brother."

Let future visitors make of those epitaphs what they will.

✠ My old bedroom. I lie on the bed and sigh happily. Wouldn't it be great if I woke up now and everything had been a bad dream? I could have a good chuckle with Dervish and Bill-E, tell them how they'd been killed off, play up the grisly circumstances of their deaths, stick some hair around my face to make me look like a werewolf.

But it's not a dream and I can't pretend that it is. Too much about me is different, not least the fact that my legs stick way out over the end of the bed, far past the point where my feet used to stop.

I look through my old clothes and CDs, remembering a time when such things were important. I go to the toilet and think about Reni Gossel, Loch's sister, as I'm washing my hands. We would have become an item if the world hadn't spun off its rails. Maybe I should look her up, kiss her farewell, tell her something corny, like I'll always hold her dear to my heart.

Then I catch sight of my twisted face in the mirror, the fangs, the bloodshot eyes, the tufts of coarse hair, the way one ear sticks out about two inches higher than the other. Some boyfriend I'd make in this state! Best to give Reni a wide berth. I'd terrify her if she saw me like this, and I didn't come back to freak out my ex-girlfriend.

Why did *you come?* the Kah-Gash asks. The voice of the ancient weapon usually speaks to me only when the situation is dire. But its curiosity has been aroused.

"To say goodbye," I tell it. "I want to see the old place one last time. Kirilli was right—houses are like people. I want to let the mansion know how much it meant to me."

Very peculiar, the Kah-Gash says drily. *I thought you had put such quaint human ways behind you forever.*

"I thought so too," I mutter, then wink at myself in the mirror. "But I'm glad that I haven't."

I head for the ground floor. The others are drinking in the kitchen, Kernel and Kirilli from glasses, Curly and Moe from bowls. I tell them I'll be a few more minutes, then steel myself and open the door to the cellar.

Dervish's wine collection—his pride and joy—is a mess. Lots of the racks have been knocked over, and hundreds of bottles lie smashed on the ground, their contents spilled. I was never bothered about wine, but I feel sad viewing the destruction, knowing how rare some of the bottles were and how much they meant to my uncle.

Stepping carefully through the wreckage, I open the secret panel that nestles behind a fake wine rack. I trudge down a long tunnel to the house's second, secret cellar. This was where Dervish cast his more dangerous spells and communed with Lord Loss.

There's magic in this room. I never asked Dervish where it came from. Maybe it has something to do with the lodestone buried in the cave not far from here.

I use my power to light the candles dotting the walls. The room flickers into view, and my eyes are drawn to the remains of a steel cage. We kept Bill-E in it when he was turning. I was a prisoner there too for a while. Hard to believe such puny bars could ever have held the likes of me. But I wasn't a monster in those days.

I wander around the cellar, looking at the books, the scraps of burned paper, the chess pieces left over from when we challenged Lord Loss. I never liked this room, but it doesn't scare me as it once did. Nothing really scares me now. Except the thought of Bec collaborating with the demons, or me destroying the universe. Heh!

A book among the debris catches my attention. There's

a picture of Lord Loss on the cover. I pick it up and study the demon master. My lips curl. Of all the monsters, this is the one I hate most. I'd give anything to look in his eyes and laugh as I throttled the life out of him. I'd maybe even accept defeat in the war if I could settle the score with this lowly one first.

As I'm thinking about Lord Loss, the picture moves. His eyes come into focus and he leers. "Grubitsch..." he whispers. "Come to me...Grubitsch..."

"In my own good time," I growl.

The face presses out of the page like a 3-D image. "Give yourself...to me. Let me end...it all now. No more pain. No more sorrow. No more—"

"—of your bull," I snort, then roar at the book. Lord Loss's face wrinkles, then flattens. Seconds later it's just a picture, and his voice is gone. I toss the book aside. "That's enough nostalgic crap," I huff, and head back to the house, all my goodbyes completed, ready for business.

ROCK ON

✠　✠　✠

WE walk to the cave, leaving the pilot and the helicopter at the house. I know this forest so well, even having been away so long, that I could go through it with my eyes closed and never stumble. I savor the familiar sights and smells, taking it all in. I sense things kicking into high gear. This could be my last quiet night for a long time, maybe ever.

When we reach the place where the cave is, there's no sign of an entrance.

"What's happening?" Kernel asks, sniffing the air uneasily.

"The hole's been filled," I tell him.

"Then we've nothing to worry about," he says. "They can't do anything with the lodestone unless they can access the cave from this side."

"I'm not taking any chances." I grab Kernel's hand and squeeze hard. As he yelps, I use the power of the Kah-Gash to unite with him. Our potential skyrockets, and I draw energy from everything around us, and from the reservoir of magic beneath our feet.

With my free hand, I point at the spot where the hole used to be and bark a command. Rocks and dirt—along with lots of insects and a few startled rabbits—fly into the air in a funnel and arc over our heads.

Kernel trembles when I release him. "How did you do that?" he croaks. "You took power from me without my permission."

"I'm the trigger," I remind him. "The guy who fires the Kah-Gash into life. I don't need permission."

"So you can steal from me whenever you like," Kernel snarls, relations between us deteriorating as swiftly as they'd started to improve.

"Don't have a heart attack," I mutter, then scramble down the hole into the gloom of the subterranean world.

Kirilli helps Kernel as we climb down a steep wall. Moe and Curly flank them, growling softly, wary of this underground den. I'd be happy to descend in the dark, but Kirilli creates a ball of light. "There," he beams. "That's much better."

As he says that, his prosthetic foot slips and he drops. A yell escapes his lips, and his eyes widen with alarm. But before he can plummet to his death, Moe grabs his left arm. The werewolf braces himself and clings to the wall as Kirilli jolts about. Once the startled magician has regained his wits—along with his grip—Moe lets go.

"He saved my life," Kirilli gasps, looking like he's about to be sick. "These beasts are becoming more human every day."

"Don't bet on it," I grunt. "He only kept you alive in case he gets hungry later."

Kirilli chuckles weakly. "You're joking, right, Grubbs?" I carry on climbing down. "*Grubbs?*"

✠ The cave hasn't changed since the night Bill-E died. I can still appreciate its spectacular beauty, the amazing array of stalagmites and stalactites, the unusual formations, the waterfall cascading from one of the walls. That surprises me. After everything that happened, and all the wonders I've seen in the demon universe, I thought I'd be immune to the charms of the cave. But it thrills me almost as much now as when I first discovered it with Bill-E and Loch.

"Impressive," Kirilli murmurs, strolling through the fields of stalagmites. "I did a bit of spelunking in my younger days. This is a splendid fissure. I'm sure it's the start of a chain of caves. If I had the proper equipment, I'd love to explore fully."

"We're not here to map cave systems," I growl, marching over to the waterfall. I squint at the wall around it. There's a thin crack that was once much larger. That was where the tunnel would have opened if the demons had been successful.

"Kernel," I call. He approaches warily, guided by Kirilli. I gouged out his eyes in a cave. I'm sure he's thinking about that now, wondering if I plan to slice off any more body parts. "I want to link up with you again. Do I have your *permission?*"

"You'd do it even if I refused," Kernel sneers, but sticks out a hand.

Using the Kah-Gash, I power up, then roar at the cave wall, the same way that I roared at the picture of Lord Loss in the cellar. The rock quivers, like it would in an earthquake. The crack splits further, widening until it's a six-foot-high chasm. I let the roar die away, and the wall stops shaking, but the gap remains.

"Do you think this might be part of Bec's plan?" Kernel asks as I step forward. I freeze and glance back. He's smiling angelically. This isn't something he just thought of. He's been saving it to hit me with at the most distracting moment.

"What are you talking about?" I snap.

"Maybe she orchestrated the dream," he says sweetly. "For all we know, the other lodestones might not be suitable. Maybe they can only manipulate this one, and she needed you to clear the way."

I stare hatefully at the bald teenager. Right now, I'm glad I popped his eyes. I just wish I'd ripped his tongue out too.

"I guarantee one thing," I say stiffly. "If they attack, and I think all is lost, I'll toss you to my werewolves before I die."

Kernel laughs, then sticks out his hand again. "Lead on, sweet prince."

"Get stuffed," I spit, leaving him for Kirilli. Tensing, I crouch, then jump and grab hold of the bottom of the crack. Dragging myself up, I peer into the darkness. I can't see or hear anything, but Kernel's warning has unsettled me, and I stand guard as the others climb, not wanting to venture farther without backup.

When we're all gathered in the mouth of the tunnel, we

advance. It's hotter than the cave, and even though it's wide enough for a couple to walk side by side, I keep imagining the walls grinding shut, pulping us to mincemeat. Kirilli and Kernel are nervous too, while Moe and Curly whine unhappily as they trudge along reluctantly.

Eventually the tunnel opens out into another cave. There's a lake of calm, clear water covering most of the floor. In the center stands an island of bones, on top of which rests a large, jagged chunk of rock—the lodestone.

"I'm not a good swimmer," Kirilli says uncertainly.

"I doubt if it's deep," I say, striding into the water. Even with my hairy legs, it feels cold.

"Should we undress?" Kirilli asks.

"Don't bother."

"But if we have to walk around all night in wet clothes…"

"You're a mage," I remind him. "You can dry them off once we get out."

"Oh," he says brightly. "I forget sometimes." Chuckling, he leads Kernel into the lake. His chuckles turn to yelps when he feels the icy bite of the water, but he presses on. Curly and Moe start to follow. Then Moe splashes Curly. She yelps and splashes him back. Within moments they're involved in a water fight, rolling around, wrestling and dunking each other, barking like a pair of puppies.

I reach the island and climb onto the mound of bones. A brittle skull cracks beneath my feet. I almost apologize, but there's no point. The person this belonged to passed far beyond the need for apologies centuries before I was born.

Kernel and Kirilli climb out of the lake as I study the rock in the middle of the bones. It's rectangular, rough around the edges. A skeleton is propped against it, kneeling, its skull resting on the top. I guess these are the remains of someone whose throat was slit over the rock—lodestones need blood to thrive.

"What's it like?" Kernel asks.

"Nothing special. I've seen better in the local quarry." I push the skeleton out of the way and rub my hands together. "Down to business. Beranabus simply broke the lodestone on the ship, right? No spells or magic required, just brute force?"

"This might be different," Kernel says. "I think it's a more powerful stone."

"Only one way to find out." I grab hold of the rock. I'm expecting a shock of energy to shoot through me, but although I can feel the buzz of Old magic in the stone, it doesn't affect me. I let my fingers wander and find cracks and holds. Then I take a firm grip and strain, trying to snap the rock in two.

Nothing happens. I release the stone and scowl. "Think you're tough?" I growl. "You won't get the better of Grubbs Grady." I get hold of it again and strain once more.

"He's talking to rocks now," Kernel says.

"A definite lunatic," Kirilli purrs.

I ignore them and brace my muscles. The stone continues to resist. Losing patience, I pick it up, look around, then plow into the water, holding the rock over one shoulder. My legs buckle, and I use magic to steady them. Moe and Curly gape at me as I stagger past. The lodestone weighs me down, even though I'm using magic to support it. A few more seconds and it will drive me under the water. That wouldn't be the best way to go—pinned beneath a stone to drown.

With a savage curse, I swing the lodestone around, raise it over my head, then hurl it at the wall of the cave. The rock slams into the wall and shatters. Shards litter the floor, and chunks bounce off and rain down on the underground lake. The werewolves howl at the echoing retorts, and the cave fills with waves of noise. I crawl out of the lake, pick up the larger fragments of the lodestone, and hammer them into the wall or off each other, reducing the rock to dust. This is one stone Bec and Lord Loss won't be able to use. No tunnel will ever be opened in Carcery Vale again.

When I'm done, I lean against the wall and look around, panting. Kernel and Kirilli are wading through the lake. Moe and Curly have climbed out and are drip-drying. The island of bones looks far less menacing now. I think about dismantling it and scattering the bones. I don't have time to bury them all, but I could hide them in the lake, grant the dead at least that small measure of privacy.

As I'm deciding whether or not to set to work on the island, I hear footsteps in the tunnel. I spring away from the wall and land in the lake close to where Kernel and Kirilli were about to step out. "Wait!" I hiss, holding up a hand for silence. I listen closely, hoping I was wrong about the footsteps. But a few seconds later I hear them again. Two sets, edging closer slowly, cautiously.

"Company?" Kernel whispers.

"Trouble, most likely." I bark softly at Moe and Curly. Obeying my command, they move to the mouth of the tunnel and take up position, one on either side.

"Shall I douse the light?" Kirilli asks. He's trembling. It might be from the chill of the water, though I suspect fear plays more of a part.

"No," I tell him. "When I give the order, intensify it and direct the rays at whatever comes through. If they have eyes, maybe we can blind them."

"You're good at that," Kernel mutters sarcastically.

We fall silent. The footsteps draw closer. Then I see shadows. Two separate figures, one tall and skinny, the other shorter but broad. The tall, skinny one might be the shadow of Lord Loss, but the other can't be Bec. Not unless she's chosen a new form, like Nadia Moore did when she joined the demon master.

Their feet come into view. I see boots and the hems of trousers. They both look human. Soldiers perhaps, sent to assassinate us? Mages? Spelunkers, like the young Kirilli Kovacs? Some chance of that!

The pair pause, perhaps sensing trouble. Then the broader one shrugs and steps forward quickly, the taller one taking a hasty stride to keep up. Curly and Moe howl and leap, claws extended.

"No!" I roar, and they wheel away instantly.

The two humans were raising guns in self-defense, but now they lower them and stare at us.

"Who is it?" Kernel hisses, fingers twitching. "What's going on?"

"It's me," the broad one says.

"And me," the lankier one adds.

"Shark?" Kernel gasps.

"Yeah," the soldier grunts.

"And Timas Brauss," the computer whiz says.

Shark looks at the werewolves, the island of bones, the shattered lodestone, and the three of us shivering in the water. Then he grins. "So," he drawls, "have you missed me?"

SHARK ATTACK

✠ ✠ ✠

THE last time I saw Shark was just after we escaped from Wolf Island. He'd been mauled by werewolves. Any normal person would have died from his wounds, but Shark is as stubborn as they come. He refused to roll over and die.

He's still in bad shape. His left ear was bitten off and a raw-looking stump remains. He can see out of his right eye, but only just—the flesh around it is scarred and pink. All four fingers on his left hand were severed, leaving the thumb looking lonely and strange. The thumb and index finger on his right hand are gone too. And he's wearing a brace from his waist to just beneath his chest.

"You look like hell," I roar happily, picking him up and swinging him around.

"Mind the ribs," he wheezes, and I immediately put him down. He scowls at me. "You don't look any great shakes yourself. Haven't you heard of razors?"

"No time for shaving. I've been too busy killing demons."

"That's no excuse," he says, then winks with his good eye.

"Hi," Kernel says, shuffling forward and extending a hand.

"How you doing, kid?" Shark asks with unusual kindness, ignoring the hand and giving Kernel a hug.

"Surviving," Kernel sighs.

"I'm Kirilli Kovacs," the stage magician introduces himself, straightening like a soldier presenting himself to an officer. "I'm a Disciple."

"That so?" Shark grunts, running a bemused eye over Kirilli's costume.

"Nobody has to bother with me," Timas says cheerily. "I don't matter."

"Of course you do," I chuckle, moving forward to shake the hand of the tall, thin, red-haired computer genius.

"I was eagerly looking forward to seeing you again," Timas says. "Primarily, I must admit, because of the chance to renew my relationship with the delicious Meera Flame. But I understand she has been taken from us."

"About a month ago," I nod, my smile fading as I recall her grisly death. "She took Juni Swan with her. Blew her into a thousand lumpy pieces."

"Some small comfort," Timas says. "I have been seeking solace in the world of computers, but since Meera I find it hard to summon up the same enthusiasm as before. I think I might be in mourning. Or perhaps it's just that I changed my diet recently."

Kirilli raises an eyebrow. I smile and whirl my finger around beside my head.

"What have you two been up to?" I ask. "It feels like years since Wolf Island."

"I've been recovering," Shark says gruffly, hating to admit to his wounds.

"And I've been playing nursemaid," says Timas.

"I wanted to join up with you earlier, but my doctor wouldn't let me," Shark complains. "She kept me sedated. I'd be there still if she hadn't been eaten by a demon. Her replacement was less concerned about me."

"Are you sure you're OK?" I frown. "I don't want you dropping dead on us."

"Some hope! I've been in a couple of fights already. I wanted to limber up before I tracked you down, make sure everything was in working order. As dozens of dead demons would tell you if they could talk — it is."

"How do you fight with so few fingers?" Kirilli asks.

Shark bends his thumb. "I gouge." Kirilli laughs, but stops when he realizes Shark is serious. The ex-soldier glares at Kirilli, then turns his gaze to me. "What about you? Anything new I need to know?"

"Yeah. But let's go back to the other cave. The skulls and bones are giving me the creeps."

"You're getting soft," Shark snorts, but follows me up the tunnel to the cave of natural wonders.

As we settle down close to the waterfall, we fill Shark in on all that's been going on. Kirilli tells him what happened on the ship of zombies. Kernel gives him a quick rundown of his trip across the universe with the Old Creatures. Then I describe our battle with Death and the demons. When I get to the bit about Kernel's eyes, Shark interrupts forcefully.

"What the hell do you mean?" he shouts, staring from me to Kernel. "I assumed some demon blinded him. Are you seriously telling me *you* did it?"

"I had to," I mutter. "He was going to leave."

"So what?" Shark roars. "He's one of us. You never turn on your own."

"See?" Kernel smiles tightly. "That's what I've been saying for a month."

"You don't understand." I hate the way Shark looks at me. "We're up against *Death*. We can't beat it by normal means. Our only hope is the Kah-Gash. If Kernel leaves, we're finished. I need him to help me find Bec and unleash the full power of the weapon."

"I keep telling you there's no hope," Kernel snaps. "I won't waste my time fighting a losing battle. Even if you could convince me to stay, we'd still need Bec, but now that she's turned against us..."

"What are you talking about?" Shark frowns.

I tell him about my dream, how I saw Bec ally herself with Lord Loss. "She vowed to lead him to the lodestones. With the help of those, he can create tunnels between universes."

"What makes you think it wasn't just a nightmare?" Shark asks.

"This was no ordinary dream. It's real, trust me."

"Let me get this straight," Shark says grimly. "You three are the Kah-Gash, the most powerful weapon ever. One of you has turned into a savage werewolf, the second wants to quit and head for the far side of the universe, and the third appears to be a traitor. You guys are supposed to be our best hope? Sounds to me like we'd be better off without the whole damn lot of you!"

"We're doomed without the Kah-Gash," I retort. "The demons will wash over us. Earth won't see out the year."

"At least we won't be torn to shreds by our *friends*," Shark fires back at me. "I'd rather be gutted by a demon than stabbed in the back by you."

My temper flares and I lean forward menacingly, growling. Moe and Curly lean in beside me—any foe of mine is an enemy of theirs.

"Easy, doggies," Shark murmurs, making soothing gestures with his mangled hands.

"Don't bait me," I snarl. "I'm not in the mood to be insulted."

"I don't care about your mood," Shark says. "You're putting yourself forward as our champion, but I think the wires in your head have got crossed. Hell, even Timas seems normal compared to you."

"I object to that slur on my good character," Timas says, but Shark ignores him.

"I'm serious, Grubbs. It takes a lot to scare me, but listening to you and seeing that crazy look in your eyes...I'm not sure you're in control anymore."

"I'm in full control," I say through clenched teeth. "I didn't enjoy blinding Kernel, but it needed to be done. You've done things you didn't like in the past, so don't get high and mighty with me. I couldn't have faced this as a human—I was weak. Now I'm strong and heartless, like the demons. I can do whatever it takes to save the world."

"You reckon?"

"Yes."

"You're afraid of nothing, ready to face anything the Demonata can throw at you?"

"Damn straight."

Shark smiles icily. "Then why haven't you gone after Bec?"

I blink. "I had to come here first, to destroy the lodestone."

Shark shakes his head. "There are other stones. Bec might be revealing their location to Lord Loss even as we speak. You should have targeted *her*."

"I thought she'd come here," I mumble. "This was one of the most powerful stones. They've used it before, so I figured—"

"Bull!" Shark stops me. "You came here to stall for time because you're afraid. I see it in your eyes, inhuman as they are. You can't mask the traces of fear, not from those who know what to look for."

"What the hell do you know about fear?" I challenge him hotly.

"More than I ever wished to," Shark says softly. "I've lived with real terror, as have most of us who fight these demonic beasts. I've seen horror in my eyes when I've woken in the middle of the night and looked in a mirror. Hell, I've seen it in daylight too. I don't let fear distract me, but it's always there. It's in you too. And I think it's misleading you."

I start to roar a denial...then stop.

He's right. As soon as he says it, I know. Shark isn't the most vocal of people, but he has the knack of hitting the nail clean on the head when he does speak up. I *am* afraid. Not of the Demonata or Bec, but of myself and Juni's prophecy that I'd destroy the world.

I should have gone after Bec once I'd recovered from my wounds. I could have let Kernel leave, just asked him to locate Bec and open a window before he went. I don't truly believe we can defeat Death, even with all three pieces of the Kah-Gash. People wiser than me have said it's impossible, and I'm sure they're correct.

I kept Kernel because I was afraid. I didn't want to go after Bec. I preferred to carry on fighting, doing what I was good at—what I was *safe* at. If I'd let Kernel go, it would have meant returning to the demon universe and running the risk of becoming a world-destroying monster. By staying here, I childishly hoped to avoid my destiny. It was a delaying measure, nothing more.

I thought I was Grubbs Grady—superhero. But I've been trying to hide from the universe—from myself—ever since our escape from Lord Loss and his army. Now that Shark's opened my eyes to the truth, I know it's time to stop.

"Kernel, I'm sorry," I mutter. His features crease with surprise. "I was wrong. I was cowardly. I was vicious."

"Keep going," he says.

"I won't hold you any longer," I tell him. "I'll take us back to the Demonata universe and set you free. All I ask is that you locate Bec and open a window for us before you leave. I hope you'll come with us, to rescue her if we can, kill her if we must, but I won't force you. It's your choice."

"If I thought we could make a difference..." he says miserably.

"You don't have to explain." Cracking my fingers, I shoot Shark a wry glance. "You should have been a psychologist."

"And put up with whining brats like you every day? No thanks."

"Excuse me for pointing out the obvious," Kirilli says, "but isn't Kernel the only one of us who can open windows?"

"No," I say. "I can too, just nowhere near as easily as him, and only to a single place in the demon universe. It'll take a few hours, but we're in an area of magic, so I'll be able to tap into that energy."

"There would have been much more magic to tap into if you hadn't destroyed the lodestone," Kirilli murmurs.

I lean in close. "See those werewolves?" I hold my thumb and index finger a quarter of an inch apart. "I'm this close to serving you to them for lunch."

As Kirilli blanches, I close my eyes and draw all the power that I can from the air. It's fading now that the lodestone's been smashed, but I don't give the stage magician the satisfaction of telling him he was right. Taking a deep breath, I recall the first line of the spells that Beranabus taught me, and begin.

WHO'S THAT GIRL?

�֝   �֝   ✖

Iᴛ takes longer than I thought it would to open the window, and it's bloody uncomfortable. Kernel makes it look easy— he just moves his hands around and voilà! Even Beranabus was able to open one with relative ease. But I operate more like Dervish did when he once summoned Lord Loss in the cellar at Carcery Vale. Lots of huffing and puffing, incantations, smoke steaming out of my pores.

Finally, after hours of intense effort, a weak-looking window of yellow light forms. "Quick," I groan at the others. "I don't know how long it will last."

Shark is first through. He moves stiffly, hindered by his brace, and looks quite pitiful, but I wouldn't like to be the demon who mistakes Shark for an easy target. Timas hurries after him. I don't think he'll be much use over there—he has all the magical talent of a slug—but he won't abandon Shark.

Kirilli hesitates. "Maybe one of us should stay here to..." He stops, unable to think of a valid excuse.

"Cower?" I suggest.

Kirilli shoots me a dark look, then steps through. I bark at Moe and Curly and they cross. Then I take Kernel's hand and lead him to the window. He pauses in front of it.

"I can still sense the lights," he whispers, moving his head as if he had eyes.

"I bet my window doesn't compare with any of yours."

"No." He smiles. "But you did good for a novice."

He steps into the window, sighing happily, and disappears.

Are you sure this is wise? the Kah-Gash asks as I lift my leg to cross.

I frown. "You don't want me to go?"

My wants are yours, the voice of the ancient weapon says. *I have always served, hiding myself when you wished, fighting your wolfen half when you were afraid of it, helping you take the world back through time when the Demonata crossed. You don't trust me, but I have always respected your desires.*

"Then tell me if this is the right thing to do."

I cannot judge. I merely question your actions because I sense your uncertainty.

"Will I destroy the world if I go after Bec?" I press. "Should I flee with Kernel to the other side of the universe? Throw myself off a cliff?"

I don't know, the Kah-Gash says. *I have no insight into the future. I only know that you mistrust this course, so I ask as your friend—is this wise?*

"You want me to find her, so we can unite and set you free," I challenge it.

I have always been free, the Kah-Gash retorts. *I choose my hosts and stay of my own free will.*

"But you want to be made whole again?"

There's silence for a few seconds. Then a sigh. *The window is about to close. Cross or stay, the choice is yours. But choose now.*

I want to question it further, but there isn't time. Cursing, knowing this might be the worst move I ever make, I throw myself through the window just before it blinks out, severing the link between universes.

✠ We're in the middle of an oasis. At least that's what it looks like, but on closer examination you can see that the trees are made of bones and scraps of human skin, and the pool at the center is alive and carnivorous. This was one of Beranabus's favorite spots in this foul universe. He often rested here.

"What kept you?" Shark asks.

At the same time Kernel says, "We shouldn't be here."

"I was tying my shoelaces," I tell Shark, then turn to answer Kernel.

"You're not wearing any shoes," Shark notes.

"You're *so* observant," I respond drily.

"Bec knows about this place," Kernel says, raising his voice. "We stayed here after the attack at the hospital. She might be keeping tabs on it."

"I already thought of that," I scowl, "but this is the only place Beranabus showed me how to get to. I couldn't guide us anywhere else."

"That's stupid," Kernel barks. "The location is irrelevant. You could have—"

"You can stand there and lecture me," I snap, "or you can build a fresh pair of eyes and lead us all to safety."

Kernel grumbles, but turns, sits, and focuses on his empty sockets. As he directs magic at the place where his eyes once were, Moe growls and advances on him, followed by Curly.

"Easy," I soothe them. "Change of plan. Let him work on the eyes."

The werewolves stare at me. Sighing, I thicken the cords in my throat and growl their new instructions. Once the message has penetrated, they explore the trees around us, chasing each other through them, munching strips of flesh and breaking off bones to gnaw.

"Is the water safe to drink?" Kirilli asks, stepping towards the dark pool.

"It's not water," I tell him. "If you get close, it will pull you in and eat you."

"Nice," Shark grunts. "You know how to pick the perfect spot for a date."

"Are there any computers here?" Timas asks, studying the trees.

"This is the universe of the Demonata," I remind him. "The home of magic and monsters, nightmares and madness. Of course there are no bloody computers!"

"Why not?" he asks. "Maybe demons like to surf the web too."

I roll my eyes, but inside I'm smiling. They're a weird,

wounded lot, but I can rely on every one of them to stand by me in a fight. Well, maybe not Kirilli if his yellow streak kicks in... or Timas if he gets bored... or Kernel once he takes off for his rendezvous with the Old Creatures... or Shark if the brace holding his guts in place cracks open...

"What are you grinning at?" Shark asks.

"You wouldn't like it if I told you," I chuckle. To hell with the odds — at least they're my friends. If things go bad, I'd rather die in the company of this bunch of misfits than with anyone else.

✠ Kernel's still working on his eyes. They're starting to come together. At the moment they look like a runny egg that's been poured back into the two halves of its shell. The rest of us are sitting nearby. Moe and Curly lie by my feet, panting after their playful chase.

I'm in the middle of telling Shark and Timas about Beranabus's soul, how we found it inside the Shadow and freed it, what he told us before he departed. I'm interrupted by choking noises. Glancing over, I spot Curly shaking her head and retching. I grin, figuring she swallowed a bone the wrong way, but then Moe growls and edges away from her. I sense something's wrong.

"Move back," I tell the others. They shuffle away, Kernel too, knowing better than to question me. Moe is snarling, his teeth bared, eyeing Curly darkly.

The female werewolf rolls around, whining and gasping. I howl a question, but she either doesn't hear or can't respond. She's clawing at her face. I howl again, trying to calm her, but she staggers to her feet and whirls away, making horrible sounds. She crashes into a tree, rebounds, and picks up speed. She's unconsciously heading for the pool. I see the liquid draw towards the edge closest to us. It senses a victim and is getting ready to pounce.

I race after the distressed werewolf and tackle her. She lashes out at me, but feebly, no power in the punch. I get a glimpse of her face and shudder. Her flesh is bubbling as if she's been dunked in a bucket of acid. Her eyes bulge, and her tongue swishes madly from one side of her mouth to the other.

"What's wrong with her?" Kirilli yells.

"Damned if I know," I mutter, nudging her away from the pool, ready to defend myself if she attacks.

Curly lurches to her knees, then throws herself down and buries her face in the soil. She thrashes wildly, sending clouds of dust shooting into the air. She slams her face harder into the ground, as if she wants to destroy it.

Curly screams, squeezes her head, then slumps. Her hands fall away. Her legs shiver, then go still. She lies facedown, breathing shallowly, silent. I edge closer, wary, expecting her to leap up and attack. But she's not playing possum. She doesn't move as I poke her with my right foot, or when I kneel beside her and pull her head up by her hair.

There are gasps from the others when they see her face. I frown at them, then rotate her head. As her face swings into view, I see what disturbed them. Her features have altered. There's another face poking out of the flesh and bones. It's still forming, the skin around the cheeks bulging and warping. But I recognize it in spite of all the blood and goo.

"Bec!"

Her eyes snap open and focus on me. I almost drop her and stamp her head into the ground. But that wouldn't achieve anything. This isn't the real Bec, merely a projection. I might as well hear her out. If I do any damage, I'll only hurt Curly.

Bec's lips move and she spits out clumps of Curly's hairy flesh. She tries to speak. Blood gurgles in her throat and she chokes. Spits it out, then retches. Curly's hand twitches and rises towards her mouth. It's probably just to wipe blood away, but I'm taking no chances. I pin her with a wrestling move and clamp her hands behind her back. There are now only inches between my face and Bec's. I draw back slightly, in case she bites.

"You don't look worried," Bec says, her voice rougher than usual, a bit of Curly's growly tone mixed in with it.

"I've seen a lot weirder than this," I shrug.

"Is that really Bec?" Shark barks.

"Quiet," I tell him.

"We should kill her if—"

"Shut up!" I roar.

Bec smiles crookedly. "You've been spying on me. I thought I sensed you, but I wasn't certain until now. You'd be more concerned if my appearance had come as a complete surprise. Will you try to kill me, Grubbs, or do you still hold out hope of reassembling the Kah-Gash?"

"What have you done?" I growl. "Have you pledged yourself to that foul hunk of rotting demon meat?"

"We can't beat them," she sighs. "Everybody realizes that except you."

"So we join them instead?" I sneer. "Never. I'd rather die than fight beside the likes of Lord Loss."

"I tried death," Bec says. "It wasn't much fun."

"Are you having more *fun* now?" I want to pound her face to bits, but it wouldn't change anything.

"Enjoyment isn't an issue any longer," Bec says. "I won't become a shrieking harpy like Juni Swan. I take no pleasure from this. But I want to survive. There's no point sacrificing ourselves when the fight has already been lost."

"Of course there is," I protest. "Dying for the people you care about has always been the ultimate point."

"But who do *you* care about?" Bec asks softly. "Your parents and Dervish are dead. Your sister, Bill-E, Meera, Sharmila. Who's left? Who are you fighting for? I think you're only resisting because it's expected. You've never looked around and said, 'I don't have to do this.' Try it, Grubbs. Ask who you fight for. Then tell me I'm wrong for choosing life over a pointless death."

I shake my head. The scary thing is, it's tempting. I could easily accept everything she's said, choose the same way she has, abandon the post of protector that Beranabus saddled me with, ride off into a gleeful, savage sunset with Bec and Lord Loss. I never wanted to be a hero. Why die miserably when I could live triumphantly? All it takes is a slight adjustment in the way I think, and . . .

"No," I whisper, putting temptation behind me.

Bec smiles. "I almost had you for a moment, didn't I?"

"Almost," I admit, chuckling wolfishly.

"Grubbs," Kernel says.

"Not now," I snap, staying focused on Bec. "What else do you have to say? I doubt you went to all this trouble just to tempt me."

"I wanted to warn you," Bec says. "I feel I owe you that much."

"Warn me of what?" I frown.

"Grubbs!" Kernel yells. "A window is opening. I can feel it."

"*That*," Bec says sadly. Then her face freezes, turns a paler shade, and starts to disintegrate.

I drop Curly's head, lurch to my feet, and scan the surrounding area. I can't see anything, but I don't doubt Kernel. "Your eyes!" I shout.

"Not finished," he says.

"Do I have time to open a window back to Earth?"

He shakes his head.

"Then get ready to fight."

As soon as I've said it, a dark, grey window snaps into existence and hordes of Lord Loss's familiars spill through. They overrun the oasis in seconds, screaming and spitting, bearing down on us in a blast of frothing, demonic hellfire.

UNSTILL WATERS

✠ ✠ ✠

I'M driven to the ground by gibbering demons, but back on my feet moments later, scattering the beasts with a burst of magic. I look over their heads, searching for Lord Loss. The familiars don't bother me—I'm far stronger than them—but their master is a different matter. If he crosses, we're in real trouble.

But there's no sign of the eight-armed sentinel of sorrow. Demons are spilling through the window, but only underlings. Maybe he's saving his grand appearance for the end, to make more of an impression. Or maybe he's wary of Kernel and me, and wants to see how we fare against his familiars first.

Several small, furry demons attack the blind teenager. They have long snouts with suckerlike mouths at the end. I think their orders were to focus on his eyes if he'd reconstructed them.

"Kernel!" I roar.

He bats most of them away and smashes the snouts of

another pair with a karate kick that Bruce Lee would have been proud of.

An octopus-like demon launches itself at me and wraps its tentacles around my throat. I bite through a couple—sushi...yum!—then grab one and yank the demon in hard. I head-butt it and send a thousand volts of magical electricity crackling through its brain. The octopus drops, its remaining tentacles withering. Stepping onto its carcass, I bound into the air and rain a sheet of fire down on the demons closest to me. Their screams are music to my ears.

Kirilli is warding off monsters, firing weak bolts of energy at them, yelping and staggering around anxiously. He'd be a good fighter if he could forget about his fear and just focus. Even in this agitated state, he's powerful enough to drive back the demons who attack him. His biggest worry will be tripping over his own feet and leaving himself open to assault.

Timas and Shark are fighting side by side, with their bare hands and feet. Shark prefers the old-fashioned ways, punching, kicking, throttling. He likes to get his hands—well, thumb!—dirty. Timas isn't able to do anything magical, but he's fast and sharp, and although he can't kill the demons, he repels them artfully and calmly. He wouldn't last long by himself, but with Shark by his side he holds his own.

Moe is slaughtering the stampeding creatures with delight. It's Christmas come early as far as he's concerned. He rips throats open, tears off limbs, disembowels viciously. His only regret is that he can't stop to feast on the spoils.

Curly staggers to her feet, her face a broken mess. She lasts about three miserable seconds, mewing painfully and trying to push the pieces of her cheeks back into place. Then demons drag her down and finish her off. A sad end for a fine warrior.

Five large, burly beasts slide through the window. They're giants, twelve feet tall. I get the sense that they're tough as rocks, but not much on the magical front. If these are the fiercest foes we have to deal with, it will be a breeze. It'll take a while, but we can wipe out this crowd without having to go into second gear.

I don't get it. There must be more to come, or maybe there's a hidden threat among the smaller, yapping demons. Lord Loss wouldn't waste his familiars on us. He'd happily sacrifice them if he thought they could wear us down and leave us ripe for the picking, but these guys wouldn't even test a run-of-the-mill mage.

As I'm trying to figure out the method behind his apparent madness, the giants grab the smaller demons and lob them through the air into the pool of living liquid. It bubbles and seethes, swiftly stripping the skin and burning through the bones of the familiars, dissolving the shells of the more heavily protected.

"What's going on?" Shark yells, throwing a poodlelike demon with four heads at one of the giants, who grabs it like a frisbee and spins it off into the pool, where it only has time to bark twice before its tongue is fricasseed by the foaming liquid. "They're doing our work for us."

"Maybe they're on our side," Kirilli squeals happily. "They think we're going to win the war, so they've betrayed their master and are trying to prove themselves worthy of our mercy."

"I doubt it," I mutter, head-butting another octopus demon, watching warily as more demons are thrown into the pool. The liquid's glowing with different hues of demon blood. I've a bad feeling about this.

As another demon is tossed into the ravenous pool, the liquid throbs. The giants kneel in front of the pool and bow their heads. Some of the demons attack them spitefully, but the giants ignore their blows and wait patiently, like monks praying at an altar.

The liquid throbs again, then rises up in a circular sheet of dripping darkness. It looms over the kneeling giants and lesser demons. For a mad moment I think it's going to form legs and stride towards us. But instead it crashes down over the giants and those around them, breaks like a wave, then re-forms and rises again, even larger than before.

The sheet of lethal liquid sloshes forward several yards, by means I can't work out, then collapses over another pack of demons, smothering and dissolving them, expanding again as it pulls itself up to its full, majestic height.

The pool is getting closer to us. Most of the demons have realized they're in trouble. Some try to attack the moving pool, only to be scorched and torn apart. The smarter beasts flee for their lives.

Shark, Timas, Kirilli, and Moe have clustered around me. They're all staring with disbelief at the aqueous, mobile tower. I call Kernel to our ranks, then prepare a ball of energy, taking power from Kernel and the others. I unleash it at the sheet of liquid. The ball punches a hole through the sheet and sizzles angrily as it shoots out the other side. But then the liquid oozes shut over the rip, and the pool sways on, undaunted.

"Bloody Beranabus!" I howl. "He told us the master of this realm had left or been killed. He was wrong. The pool *is* the master. It's been dormant, lacking the power to move, but now that it's been fed enough demons..."

I try a freezing spell, but although part of the pool half-frosts over for a couple of seconds, it doesn't take hold and the killer sheet presses on, destroying more of the demons, which I now realize were sent here for the sole purpose of empowering the slumbering behemoth.

"We can't defeat it," I huff, backpedaling.

"Perhaps an evaporation spell?" Kernel suggests.

"Nothing will work. It's a demon master and this is its realm."

"Surely we can outrun it," Kirilli says.

I laugh. "You can always rely on Kovacs to opt for a hasty retreat. But this time he's right. Let's make like sprinters and..."

I draw to a halt. The trees around the perimeter of the oasis are snapping together, bones and flesh linking, forming an unbroken ring. Demons screech and hurl themselves at the bony, fleshy fence, or try to scale it, but are swiftly speared by some of the longer, sharper bones.

"So much for running away," Shark sniffs. "What now, oh wise and noble leader?"

"We could offer Kirilli as a sacrifice and hope it leaves the rest of us alone," I murmur, drawing a satisfactory yelp from the terrified stage magician. "Kernel—any luck with those eyes?"

"It'll be a while," he says.

"What's taking you so long?" I growl.

"Bite me," he retorts.

The pool breaks over another group of demons. This time when it rises, it splits into two sheets, which glide apart—double trouble.

"A multiplying demon," Timas says. "Fascinating. Based on those it had to devour in order to divide once, and on those who remain…assuming it can split again…" He does a quick head count of the remaining demons. "We might have to face as many as eight clones within the next six minutes."

"We could do with a plan," Shark barks.

"I'm working on it." I look around, weighing up my options. Trying to punch a hole through the wall of bones and flesh is probably our best option. Maybe we could explode a demon against it. But I'm not convinced that will work. Demon masters make many of the rules in their own realms.

If we link, Kernel and I *might* get the better of it in a fight to the death, but again I'm dubious. Even Beranabus avoided direct confrontation with the stronger Demonata on their home turf. We'll be taking an awful risk if we pit ourselves against it.

There's one other option. The words "frying pan" and "fire" leap to mind as soon as I consider it. But if it's a choice between facing a firing squad and jumping off a cliff, I'll always opt for the jump because you might get lucky on the way down.

"Follow me!" I shout, grabbing Kernel's hand and darting forward. I narrowly dodge the pillars of liquid, racing past them as they crash to the ground less than a yard to my left. I head for the spot where the pool used to rest, and where the window that the demons crossed through is still hanging in the air.

"You've got to be joking!" Shark roars. "That leads to Lord Loss's realm!"

"That's where we were heading anyway, wasn't it?" I yell back.

"But the plan was to take him by surprise. If we jump through a window that he made..."

"Hell," I chuckle, "if I was in his shoes, and some nutcase jumped through my window and straight into my arms, it'd sure take *me* by surprise!"

Before Shark can argue, I hit the window of light and throw myself at it, bursting through, bellowing wildly, relishing the insane buzz of my suicidal lunge.

KNIGHTS IN SLIMY ARMOR

✠　　✠　　✠

NOTHING but cobwebs. I whirl wildly as the others crash through after me, sure Lord Loss and his minions are hiding in the shadows. But we're alone in a large, bare room. No time to wonder at that. I don't know if the mobile pool can cross after us, but taking no chances, I cast a spell over the window, establishing a shield to block anything else from following.

"Where is he?" Shark growls, casting an uneasy eye around the room.

"I don't know." I try sensing the demon master's presence, but I've never been good at that type of magic.

"Let's get out of here," Kirilli moans.

"Don't be stupid," I snap. "This is where we wanted to get to."

"But it's different now," Kernel says, taking Kirilli's side. "Lord Loss herded us here. It's obviously part of a plan. We'd be crazy to go on."

"That's the way it always is," I shrug. "Lord Loss sets a

trap—I blunder into it and hope for the best. So far I've got the better of him. My luck's bound to run out eventually, but there's nothing else I can do. I don't have the brains to outwit him, just the brawn and guts to fight back."

"So you want to walk into his den and take things from there?" Kernel asks.

"Yeah," I grin.

"That's madness."

"Maybe. But in my experience, the cleverer you are, the more ways you find to shoot yourself in the foot. Juni, Davida Haym, and Antoine Horwitzer were way smarter than me, and each set me up for an elaborate fall. But I'm here and they're dead. Sometimes it pays to be simple."

Kernel frowns. "In a strange way, that almost makes sense."

"Stop talking!" Kirilli shrieks. "Get us out of here!"

"We're not leaving," I growl. "Kernel, how are those eyes coming along?"

"I reckon another ten minutes if we aren't distracted."

"Coolio." I crack my knuckles. "We could wait here, but I think we're better off taking the fight to them."

"Knowing you as well as they do, that's probably what Lord Loss and Bec are counting on," Kernel warns me.

"Good. I'd hate to disappoint them. But there's a personal matter I want to settle first."

"What are you talking about?" Shark scowls.

"You'll see," I mutter, then head out of the room and set off through the castle that I've explored a few dozen times in my dreams.

�֍ Timas is intrigued by the webby mechanisms of the castle. If he had his way, we wouldn't move on until he'd made a full study of each room. But I ignore his pleas to slow down and instead plow on until I find a corridor that I remember from my nightmarish meanderings with Bec and Lord Loss.

Once I've got my bearings, I pick up speed, leading the others through a series of corridors and rooms, down into the dungeon. We encounter none of Lord Loss's familiars. That's weird—this place should be packed with nasty little demons—but I've no time to worry about it. If I don't do anything else right, there's at least one wrong I'm determined to fix. It's a minor matter in the grand scheme of things, but it's important to me.

I'm nearing the door when Kernel stops and says, "Peekaboo!"

I face the bald teenager with the caramel-colored skin. His bright blue eyes are back in place, little flickers of light dancing across his pupils. He stares at the air around me, smiling widely.

"You can still see the lights?" I ask.

"Oh yes," he breathes, extending a hand to caress an invisible patch. He parts his fingers and stares at me through the cracks. "This is where I say goodbye." He says it warily, expecting me to argue.

I nod shortly, then jerk my head at the corridor ahead of us. "Around that bend is the door to a dungeon. Lots of humans are imprisoned there. Lord Loss tortures them in his spare time. I'm going to free them. Want to help?"

"You told me I could leave," Kernel says guardedly.

"You can. But if you do and we fail, you'll condemn these captives to suffer at the hands of Lord Loss, maybe for thousands of years."

Kernel licks his lips and frowns. I almost have him.

"One of the prisoners is a girl called Bo Kooniart. She helped Dervish and me break out of Slawter. She could have left with us, but she went back to find her father. And her brother." I smile crookedly at Kernel. "She risked all to save her brother. You and I know what that's like, don't we?"

Kernel nods unhappily.

"You can tell where Lord Loss and Bec are," Shark says. "Search for them. Check if they're waiting in the dungeon for us."

Kernel studies the invisible lights for a few seconds. "They're on one of the higher levels, at the center of the castle."

"Then what are you scared of?" Shark grins.

Kernel glares at me. "One last favor, then I'm out of here. Agreed?"

"Do whatever the hell you want, baldy," I sniff and press on, hiding my smile behind a bloodstained, hairy hand.

✠ The door, like everything else, is made of cobwebs. It's the only door we've encountered in the castle. Timas bends to study the hinges as it swings open. The rest of us move forward, me first, followed by Shark, Kernel, Kirilli, and Moe. We hear the victims before we spot them, low moans, pained weepings, soft cries for mercy and death.

We fan out and Kirilli edges ahead of the rest of us, eyes

widening as he studies the humans strapped to the walls and tables, the implements of torture lying like toys across the floor and webby shelves.

"This is despicable!" he splutters.

A man with half a face lifts his head at the sound of Kirilli's voice and stares at him through one eye. "Have you come to kill us?" he wheezes.

"We've come to save you," Kirilli says, hurrying to his side.

The man sneers wearily. "Don't make fun of me. Lord Loss sent you to give us false hope."

"No, honestly," Kirilli insists, "we're here to—"

"Watch out overhead!" Timas shouts behind us.

I look up and spot a huge spider-shaped demon descending on a strand of web, fast as an eagle swooping on a rat. I lunge forward to protect Kirilli. Shark and Kernel react a split second later. But the furious stage magician doesn't need our help. Neatly sidestepping us, he points a finger at the spider and screams a phrase of magic, unleashing twin lightning bolts from his eyes.

The bolts strike the spider and it explodes, showering us with goo and slime. As I spit out the mess and wipe it from my eyes, I stare at Kirilli. He's standing rigid, finger still outstretched, features contorted with contempt.

"Nice work, Kovacs," I murmur. "But next time, try not to splatter us. If you'd waited till it was lower, you could have killed it *and* spared us the splash-back."

Kirilli blinks and stares at me, then realizes I'm joking and smiles tightly. "The way you smell, it wouldn't make much difference," he says.

"I'm liking you more and more," I laugh, slapping his back. "Now, shall we free these poor devils and send them home?"

"Hell, yes." Kirilli sets to work on the bonds imprisoning the skeptical half-faced man.

As the others dart about the dungeon, freeing the tormented humans, I hurry to the spot where Bo Kooniart has always been. My stomach lurches when I don't find her—the shackles that held her in place lie open on the floor. I turn to the captured, blond-haired Disciple whom I saw every time I trailed Bec and Lord Loss here. His expression is torn between hope and disbelief.

"Bo—the girl who was here—where is she?"

He doesn't respond, only stares, still not sure I'm real.

"The girl," I growl, pushing my face up to his.

"You're not...a demon," he croaks. "But you're not... human either. What...are you?"

"That doesn't matter. I'm here to rescue you. But where's the girl? Did Lord Loss...?" I don't finish, not daring to voice my worst fears.

"Back...there," the Disciple wheezes, nodding at a barred door behind me.

Hurrying to the bars, I spot Bo and two others chained to the floor. It's a small room filled with insects made of fire. They slither slowly across the helpless captives, leaving small, flame-filled channels in their flesh. Bo is gagged— they all are—so she can't scream, but I can see the pain and terror in her eyes.

Cursing, I rip the door off its hinges and toss it aside. Bursting into the room, I stamp on as many of the fiery insects as I can, then pull Bo and the others free and toss them out into the dungeon. Taking a deep breath, I blow on them, quenching the flames and killing the insects still burrowing across their chests, faces, and limbs. With a quick swipe of a claw, I cut the gags from their mouths. As they whimper and sob, I find clothes nearby and toss them to the naked prisoners. While they pull them on, I do what I can to heal their wounds. Then I turn to free more of the inmates.

"Wait," Bo croaks. "I've seen you before, but I don't know where." Her voice is surprisingly strong for one who's been through hell. Then again, remembering how she went back into the bedlam of Slawter to search for her father and brother, maybe I shouldn't be so surprised.

"Grubbs Grady," I grunt, letting my face change back to the way it was when she knew me.

Her eyes widen. *"Grubbs?* What happened to you? You look like..."

"...something from the cast of *Slawter,*" I grin.

"Is it a curse?" she asks. "Did the monsters do this to you?"

"Yeah," I mutter. "Something like that."

I help her to her feet. "Are you OK?"

"I don't know," she sighs. "It's been so long...years...yet I don't look old, do I?" She stares at her hands. Although they're rough and scarred and stained with blood, they're the hands of a girl, not an old crone.

"You look fine," I tell her. "You'll look even better once you've had a hot bath."

Bo frowns. "A hot bath? Here?"

"No," I say softly. "You're going home."

She starts to tremble. "Don't say it, not if it isn't true."

"It's true," I promise, then shout, "Kernel, where's that window?"

"Working on it," he calls back.

"Another minute or two," I tell her. "Then it will all be over."

Except for the impending apocalypse, the voice of the Kah-Gash adds inside my head, but I ignore it.

"Abe?" Bo asks quietly. "My dad?"

"You haven't seen them here?" She shakes her head. "Then they didn't make it out of Slawter."

Tears well in her eyes. "You're sure? There's nowhere else they might be?"

"No."

She nods sorrowfully and I marvel at the strength of humans. Despite all that she's suffered, her first thoughts are of her dead relatives. I thought I grew stronger when I became a wolfen beast, but in some ways maybe I lost more than I gained.

"It's open," Kernel calls, and ushers the first of the prisoners through a window of yellow light.

"Come with me," I tell Bo and the others, leading them towards the window. "There'll be people on the other side. They'll help."

"Aren't you coming with us?" Bo asks.

"No."

"He'll find you if you stay," she whispers. I don't need to ask whom she means.

"He won't have to. We're going after him."

"You think you can fight him?" She stares at me as if I'm mad.

"We'll give it a good shot."

She shakes her head wordlessly. Then we're at the window. Before she can think of anything to say, I gently push her through. I don't need thanks. It's enough to see her to safety. A small, unimportant triumph — but to me, it matters a lot.

The prisoners continue filing through, but some are beyond help. A grim-faced Shark takes care of those, breaking their necks, freeing their souls swiftly and painlessly. Sometimes that's the most you can do for a person.

The blond-haired Disciple pauses at the window and looks at us. "I should stay with you and fight," he mutters. "It's my job."

"You wouldn't be much good to us the state you're in," I say as kindly as I can.

"But I know how to do things."

"You've done enough," I smile. "Go home. Rest up. Recover. Take a long vacation. God knows, you've earned it."

"Before I leave," he says. "The war... who won?"

"Which war?" I frown.

"The World War."

"One or Two?"

His face blanches. "There was a *second*?"

"Go home," I tell him, insistent this time, feeling sorry for this confused man who's going to have to learn to adapt to what's left of life in the twenty-first century.

Soon they're all gone or beyond the reaches of pain, and it's just us in the dungeon. I look from Shark to Timas to

Kirilli. "If you want to leave, I'll understand. This is probably the end for anyone who pushes on with me."

"Do we look like cowards?" Shark snorts.

"Well..." I was about to say Kirilli did, but one glance at his determined face and I button my lip. The time for mocking Kirilli Kovacs has passed. He's truly one of us now. "Sorry. I guess I've seen too many movies. Let's go."

I start for the door.

"Aren't you even going to say goodbye?" Kernel asks.

"Why?" I grunt. "You're not going anywhere."

"You said I could leave," he snarls.

"You can," I chuckle, "but you won't. Walk out on a showdown with Lord Loss? Abandon us when there's still hope we can beat this thing? Leave Bec to ruin the world, knowing you could maybe have stopped her if you tried? Nuh-uh. You're going nowhere."

Kernel grumbles darkly and I feel his scowl burning a hole in the back of my neck. But I know, as I step through the doorway, that he'll follow. They all will. Hell, we're heroes—this is what we do.

SOULFUL

✠   ✠   ✠

WE creep through the corridors of the high-ceilinged castle, our footsteps muffled by the thick strands of web that serve as floorboards. We still haven't seen any demons. Maybe Lord Loss's familiars are with the demon army we fought the last time we were in this universe. But it's strange that he should choose to face us by himself. As a master, in his own realm, he can be confident of success, but it would be easier if he had hundreds of his henchthings to throw against us. Lord Loss doesn't usually take chances. Why do so now?

Kernel's busy juggling patches of light as we walk, putting the framework for a window together, so he can complete it quickly and make a swift getaway if he has to. I'm stunned that he came with us. I was bluffing when I said I was sure he'd stay. I totally expected him to leave. He's spent the last month going on about how he needs to return to the ark. Why the sudden change?

Guilty, the Kah-Gash murmurs inside my head.

"You did this?" I growl.

I'm able to nudge when the wish already exists, the Kah-Gash says. *I can't make any of you do something you don't want to, but I can tip the balance if you're in two minds. Kernel knew he should leave, but he wanted to stay. I played on his wishes and turned him from the path of reason.*

"I bet this isn't the first time you've manipulated us," I accuse it.

It's not manipulation, the Kah-Gash protests. *I merely give you the confidence, from time to time, to do that which you truly desire.*

"But it's what you desire too, isn't it? You want us to join. You're using us."

Such a suspicious mind, the Kah-Gash sighs, then falls silent.

I think about telling Kernel what the Kah-Gash said, offering him the chance to leave. That would be the decent thing. But I'm a slime-covered, hairy, mutated, wolfen beast. What the hell do I know about decency?

We push on until we come to a huge room, the largest in the castle. The floor is littered with toys, dolls, clothes, and other bits and pieces from Earth. In the center a huge chandelier hangs above a massive spider-shaped throne, both carved from webs. There's a painting of Lord Loss done in the style of Van Gogh pinned to the wall to the rear of the throne.

Lord Loss squats at the base of the throne, not quite touching the floor, head bent over a chessboard. Bec is his opponent. She sits cross-legged with her back to us. She's making a move as we enter, engrossed in the game.

"A moment, good people," Lord Loss mutters without looking up. He purses his bloodred lips, studies the chess pieces, then moves one of them. He smiles at Bec and says, "To be resumed." Then he straightens and Bec turns to face us.

"Hello, Grubbs," Bec says quietly. "Kernel. Shark. Kirilli." She nods at the tall redheaded man and the werewolf. Timas beams at her, but Moe just snarls. "Are these all you brought? I thought you'd come with an army."

"These will do," I tell her, moving closer, scanning the room for hidden threats. But it seems to be deserted except for this pair.

"Welcome back, Cornelius," Lord Loss says. "It seems like an age since your last visit. What a shame young Artery isn't here to greet you."

Kernel says nothing, but he looks like he's about to be sick. This is hard for him. Maybe the persuasive power of the Kah-Gash has faded and he's wondering what the hell he's doing here.

"No greeting for me?" Shark asks.

"You require none," Lord Loss says calmly. "You were always a bit player. One does not waste pleasantries on pawns."

"You're hurting my feelings," Shark sniffs. His gaze falls on Bec and he draws his thumb across his throat, trying to freak her. But if she's worried, she doesn't show it. Her expression hasn't changed in the slightest.

"This place is amazing," Timas says, squinting up at the chandelier, then at the painting behind the throne. "That's woven out of colored cobwebs, isn't it?"

"Yes," Lord Loss says, smiling with genuine warmth. "You're the first visitor to notice. It looks like oil on canvas from a distance, but in fact…" He draws to a halt and coughs into a fist. "We could be friends, Timas Brauss, if circumstances were different. You strike me as a man after my own heart." He runs a hand over the snake-filled hole in his chest. "So to speak."

"We freed your prisoners," Kirilli growls, brushing slime from the sleeves of his jacket.

"How daring of you," Lord Loss murmurs. "I am devastated. What shall I play with now in my idle moments?" His eyes twinkle viciously. "Perhaps I'll focus my attention on *you*, Master Kovacs."

Kirilli produces a playing card out of thin air, then rips it in two. "That's what I think of your *attention*."

Lord Loss frowns. "I was told you were of a cowardly nature. It seems I have been misinformed."

"No," Kirilli says. "The reports were accurate. But I've changed."

Moe growls at me questioningly.

"Yeah," I reply. "You're right."

"About what?" Lord Loss frowns.

"Moe thinks there's been too much talking and not enough killing." I slam my hands together and send a wave of magic shooting at the pair in front of the throne. I race after it, fangs and claws extended, readying myself for battle.

The wave of energy ruffles Bec's hair and sends a few drops of blood spraying from Lord Loss. But that's all. The demon master tuts and waves a hand at me. I crash to my knees, my mouth sealing as if glued shut, the hairs in my nostrils knitting together. I can't breathe. I slash at my lips with my claws, ripping them open, then dig a couple of fingers up my nose, breaking through the web of hairs.

As I draw a welcome breath, Moe, Shark, Timas, and Kirilli bound past. The werewolf's howling, Shark's roaring, and Kirilli's shrieking. Timas just whistles softly, as if heading out to work.

Lord Loss could repel them easily, but he lets the quartet close on him, then grapples with them, slapping them back, playing, letting them think they have a chance of defeating him. I know better. I felt his power as he stitched my lips and nose shut. I was wrong to think we had even a sliver of hope. This is his kingdom. He's unbeatable here.

I glance at Kernel. He's still working on a window, but he pauses when I catch his eye and raises an eyebrow, asking if I want him to fight. I shake my head, letting him know that he's fine as he is. Then I face Bec, who still hasn't moved. She's observing the fight with calm disinterest.

"Why?" I snarl, moving in on her, sure Lord Loss will intervene, tensing myself against whatever he throws at me.

"What option did I have?" Bec asks quietly. "The demons have won. There's no profit in dying heroically but uselessly."

I'm drawing closer. Lord Loss hasn't made any move to stop me. My mouth is wet with saliva and blood. I spit to clear it, then growl at her. "You fought in the past when it seemed hopeless."

"I was younger then," Bec sighs. "I believed in miracles.

Now I know we can't win. Bran knew that too at the end. You can't defeat Death."

"But he didn't give up," I remind her. "He tackled the Shadow and bought us time. He sacrificed his life to save you. And now you've pledged yourself to the beast he hated most of all."

"If I could save humanity by sacrificing myself, I would," Bec says quietly. "But nothing would be gained." She stands, picks up the chessboard, and holds it out to me. "This is the Board. It's what the universe was like in the beginning, and what it will soon be like again. Sixty-four zones, half for the Old Creatures, half for the Demonata. No room for humans. I don't think that's a good or a bad thing—it's just the way things are."

"No," I snap. "That will only happen if we let it. And we won't. *I* won't."

I'm within striking distance. Making a fist, I lash at her. I expect her to duck, but instead she swings up the Board and deflects my blow, then slams it into my chin, knocking my head back. That stuns me—I hadn't anticipated the small girl standing up to me in a fair fight. Before I can recover, she touches my stomach and sends a shock wave of magic crackling through my flesh.

I collapse in a ball, howling with pain. Bec cracks the Board over my head. I raise a hand to swat it away, but it smashes down hard on my knuckles, breaks the bones in my wrist, and hammers my face into the ground.

If the floor was concrete, my skull would be crushed and my brains pulped. But the webs give beneath me, so although I come up with one side of my face feeling like it's been caved in, my eye shut, blood pumping from any number of wounds, I *do* come up. I should be dead, but I'm not. And that's bad news for Bec.

Springing to my feet, I snap my teeth around her wrist. She didn't expect this rapid response. She thought she'd have time to attack me again. As Bec prepares a spell to repel me, I bite down hard and chew her hand off. She gasps and falls away, using the magic that was on her lips to cauterize the wound and numb the pain. Before she can reattach the hand, I drive for her throat, meaning to bite her head off as smoothly as her hand.

My jaws freeze and an electric shock courses through my veins. I fall away, spasming. As I thrash on the floor, I spot Lord Loss waving a stubby finger from side to side. "No, Grubitsch," he admonishes me. "I lost one assistant when Juni Swan was killed. I shall not lose another."

Shark roars and jams a hand into the hole in Lord Loss's chest. The snakes bite him, but he keeps his hand in, grabs a couple of the serpents and squeezes them to death. He tosses the corpses into Lord Loss's face. Blood spatters the demon master's eyes, momentarily blinding him.

As Lord Loss wipes the blood away, Shark, Moe, and Kirilli jump him. Timas starts to follow, then hesitates and turns instead to Bec. "Are you good at chess?" he asks.

Bec frowns. "I—"

He strikes before she gets any further, lashing out with his right foot. He looks like a gangly, awkward man, but he can move swiftly when he wishes. His foot connects with the side of Bec's head, knocking her sideways. She cries out with surprise.

As my jaws unlock, I scrabble after Bec, desperate to finish her off. Timas steps aside. I claw closer. Bec hears me before she sees me. She focuses on my hate-filled eyes and hisses like a cat. A phrase of magic bursts from her tongue. A split second later, her severed hand shoots across the floor, flicks onto her wrist, and dances feverishly as tendons, bones, and blood vessels fuse at a furious pace.

I throw myself at her, roaring wildly, but Bec flies out of reach, sliding across the floor to the nearest webby wall. When she hits it, she shimmies several feet up the wall, then glares at me from a safe height.

Lord Loss has cleared the mess from around his eyes and is back in business. He looks annoyed. Shark reaches into the demon master's chest cavity to kill a few more snakes. This time one of them darts from the gap and wriggles up his arm. He tries to slap it away, but it slides over his elbow, bites a hole in his biceps, then sinks its head into his flesh. Its body follows and it starts to disappear beneath his skin. Shark yelps and grabs the snake's tail. He falls away, tugging on the snake, screaming with pain and horror.

Moe howls louder than ever and digs his fangs into the doughy flesh of Lord Loss's stomach. He chews a chunk loose, then rips a twelve-inch strip of skin away. Lord Loss groans and half turns. Another two snakes dart from the hole in his chest and shoot at Moe's eyes. Their fangs hit before the werewolf can whirl aside, puncturing the globes. Moe shrieks and hits the floor, blind and in agony.

Kirilli backs up, isolated and trembling, looking from Moe to Shark.

"What now, little man?" Lord Loss whispers, rising in

the air before the stage magician, all eight arms extending to their fullest length.

Kirilli gulps, takes a few more steps back, then stops. "I guess this is where I pull off my masterstroke." He grins and whips out a couple of knives. He tosses them at the demon master, and they strike either side of the beast's right breast. As soon as they hit, they turn into weeds. Lord Loss laughs, then chokes as the weeds spread and burrow into his flesh. Within seconds his entire chest is a bed of suffocating greenery. The weeds wrap around his throat and climb his neck to his face, which is turning a beautiful purple color.

"Master?" Bec calls from her perch, looking troubled. I should go after her, but I'm transfixed by the sight of Lord Loss. It's incredible that he's struggling like this, especially at the hands of a Disciple as insignificant as Kirilli Kovacs. But maybe Kirilli is the ace up our sleeve. Nobody expected him to be a threat. Lord Loss probably didn't bother to shield himself as fully as he would have against the rest of us. If Kirilli can take advantage of that…

But even as I'm thinking the impossible, Lord Loss shudders, then smiles. The weeds die and peel away in dry clumps. Moments later only a thin rash remains.

"Impressive," Lord Loss acknowledges, "but hardly enough to bring down one such as I. Was that your best shot, Master Kovacs?"

"Pretty much," Kirilli sighs.

"So again I ask, what now, little man?"

Kirilli manages a shaky smile. "You kill me?"

Lord Loss nods and points a couple of arms at the mage.

"No!" I bellow, and hit the demon master with a burst of magic.

Lord Loss is knocked aside. Steadying himself, he glares at me. "Are you still alive? I thought you would have dealt with him by now, Little One."

"It's hard," Bec says softly. "They were my friends."

"I understand," Lord Loss purrs. "But you must kill at least one of them for me. To prove you are truly on my side."

My heart gives a hopeful leap. It seems Bec might still be torn between her original loyalties and the new vows she made. If she's wavering, there's a chance to save her. She hasn't crossed the final line yet. Maybe I can draw her back.

"Help us," I plead, locking gazes with the troubled-looking girl, letting my face soften and become more human. "If the three of us unite, we can kill him."

"I came back!" Kernel shouts. "I didn't need to. But I returned. For *you*."

"To kill me," Bec says sullenly.

"To rescue you," I disagree. "You haven't passed the point of no return. You can be one of us again. It makes sense to stick with your own. No matter what you do, you'll never be a demon."

"No," Bec says. "But I'm not really human either. I'm an agent of Death. I've passed beyond the ways of the living. This is all that's left for me."

"No!" I cry. "You can—"

"My people are dead," she interrupts. "Those I owed loyalty to died many centuries ago. Bran was the last. You're not part of my world. I'm tired of trying to do the right thing. When my soul didn't pass on, I unleashed Death.

In a weird kind of way, I'm its mother. Now I need to fully pledge myself to it."

Bec stretches out a hand towards the Board. It flies into her fingers and glows. Lord Loss sighs happily and rises above Shark and the others. As he floats, he waves at the walls around us and they dissolve, the strands of webs unraveling and dropping, revealing the areas previously walled off.

There are humans in the rooms around us. Thousands of people, standing frozen in place, eyes blank, arms by their sides. For a few seconds I think they're dead, but then I see their chests rising and falling as they breathe in unison.

"This looks ominous," Timas remarks.

"The Board!" Kernel yells. "Their souls are in the Board."

"Neatly tucked away," Lord Loss says, moving closer to Bec, a perverse smile lifting the corners of his mouth.

"Wait," I gasp, seeing the dark intent in Bec's eyes. "Don't do this. You're still one of us. Beranabus would hate you if he saw you now. Those are real people. There are children…"

"You're all children in my eyes," Bec says quietly. "I've lived for more than fifteen hundred years. Even your eldest are babes to me." Her face hardens. "And it's time to put the babies to bed."

"No!" I scream, feeling the bonds between us snap forever, seeing the last trace of humanity blink out of her eyes. I try to stop her, to jump and knock the Board from her hands. But Lord Loss waves and subdues me.

As Kernel lurches forward and Shark struggles with the

snake...as Kirilli stares at Bec and a frown creases Timas's forehead...as Moe writhes blindly on the ground and Lord Loss floats next to his protégée and nods encouragingly...

Bec places her right hand on the Board and sends waves of fire burning through the layer of crystal. I sense the flames billowing through all sixty-four zones. It's almost infinite inside, each zone the size of a galaxy, but the fire scorches through faster than the speed of light, destroying all in its path, demons, worlds, skies...and the souls of the people around us.

They fall in lines, bodies slumping and twitching, butchered by the sad-faced girl from the past. Thousands of innocent, defenseless humans—all murdered without mercy by pale, warped Bec.

AN UNHOLY QUARTET

✣   ✣   ✣

I roar wordlessly, filled with horror and hate. Bec's face is lit by the glow of thousands of burning souls. She looks awestruck and damned.

"My beloved," Lord Loss gurgles, running a sticky hand down the side of Bec's face. She doesn't respond. She's staring into the flickering glow of the Board, transfixed. She does nothing to stop the massacre, even as the bodies topple and writhe around us. I've never seen someone consciously turn to the path of evil. If it wasn't so sickening, I'd be fascinated.

"What the hell's going on?" Shark yells. He's torn off the snake's tail and sucked out its entrails. It's dead, but most of its body remains stuck in his arm.

"She killed them!" I scream, trying to climb up the wall after Bec. It's the only stretch of wall left, standing like a pillar in a huge, corpse-strewn room.

Shark looks at the falling humans. "No," he moans, struck hard by the appalling tragedy of it, even though he's seen so much in his time.

"We have to stop her," Kirilli says, stepping forward and flexing his fingers.

"I think it's passed beyond that," Timas says, squinting up at the Board. "A most remarkable device. I'd love to know how it works."

"I'm going to kill you," I vow, pointing a trembling finger at Bec. "You can't stay up there forever. As soon as you come down, you're dead."

Lord Loss laughs. "You're such a brute, Grubitsch. You think mindless violence is the answer to all the universe's troubles."

Bec blinks, then stares into the Board again. I don't know if she's heard anything we've said, if she's even aware of us. She watches the souls burn but takes no pleasure from the slaughter. This is destroying her. Her human emotions are burning away with the spirits of the dying.

"Why?" Kernel mutters. "It doesn't make sense."

"She wants to prove herself to her new master," I snarl.

"But Lord Loss didn't ask her to kill them," Kernel presses. "He asked her to kill one of *us*. There must be another reason why she targeted them instead of you or me."

"You were always smarter than your burly companion," Lord Loss says. "Not as clever as sly young Bec, but definitely several rungs higher up the IQ ladder than the somewhat dense Master Grady."

The last of the humans hits the ground, but the Board is still glowing. It's a dark glow and it pulses steadily, a gloomy, grey, *shadowy* throb.

"It's Death!" I shout, realization coming too late to be of any use.

Wispy tendrils rise from the Board and snake into the air around Bec. From a distance you might mistake them for smoke, but this close I can see that there's nothing natural about the sinewy strands. They have the same consistency Death had when we faced it before. It looks like our shadowy foe has found its way back. The humans were slaughtered so that Death could stitch together a new body from the fabric of their souls.

With a scream of failure, I unleash all of my power in a ball of magic. It roars towards Bec like a missile. Nothing should be able to halt or divert it. Bec should be smashed to pieces.

But Lord Loss intervenes, slides between Bec and me, and absorbs the blast. It slams him into Bec, who falls to the floor. But it doesn't destroy him. This is his realm. He can take all that I throw at him here and still bounce back.

Shark and Kirilli hurl themselves at Bec as she falls, murder in their eyes. But she's on her feet before they strike. With a lazy gesture, she sends them flying. She's still clutching the Board. More shadowy tendrils rise from the sixty-four squares and wrap themselves around her, caressing her, sliding up her throat, brushing across her lips. Her mouth opens and she inhales. The shadows slip down her throat, and her eyes take on a darker, more menacing color.

"Grubbs," she says, and the word rolls flatly from her mouth. "Come to me."

There's something commanding and seductive in her tone. I know she plans to kill me, but that doesn't seem like such a bad thing. If I give myself to her, it will all be over in an instant. No more pain, guilt, or suffering. One hug from the girl encased in shadows and I can join with her, become part of that gloomy subworld, seek refuge in oblivion.

"Grubbs!" Kernel shrieks. I frown at him and start to tell him not to disturb me. But then I spot a window of red light. He's opened a way out.

"I don't think so," Lord Loss snarls. He tries to intercede, but although I didn't seriously injure him when I unleashed the ball of energy, I stung him. He's slower than normal. Shark and Kirilli flee ahead of the demon master and stumble through the window. Timas takes his time, watching the Board and the way the shadows stream from it and dance across Bec's flesh. A cloud of shadows is forming around and behind her. Timas looks like he'd be happy to dive into the heart of that cloud and lose himself in it.

"Come on!" Kernel roars. "I won't wait any longer. Come now or stay and die."

Timas sighs, his shoulders slumping. He shoots Kernel a scowl, then slips through the window instead of into the cloud of shadows, choosing life over death. It's a choice I haven't made yet.

"Come to me, Grubbs," Bec whispers, and staggers forward, raising a dark hand. She tries to smile, but it's as if she's forgotten how.

"Don't kill him," Lord Loss pleads, real longing in his voice. "You said you'd let *me* murder this one. You gave your word. It was all I asked for."

"Grubbs!" Kernel yells warningly.

We can keep him, the voice of the Kah-Gash says. *We can block his retreat and hold him here. Take him into the cloud with us. All three pieces reunited by Death, a union of the* most powerful forces in the universes, a quartet instead of a trinity. It would mean power beyond all measure. You're the trigger. You can make it happen.

"Power...," I murmur, eyes wide, torn in ways I don't fully understand.

"To hell with you," Kernel sobs, then steps up to the window of red light.

I extend a hand to hold him back...then pause and let him go.

"No," I croak, my mind clearing. "I don't want this."

Bec hisses, her semi-smile crumbling. "Come to me," she growls. Not a plea this time. An order.

"Get stuffed!" I snort, then throw myself at the window. The cheated howls of Bec and Lord Loss echo after me as shadowy tendrils shoot towards me, trying to haul me back. But Death is too slow for this fleet-footed wolfen boy. I'm gone before it can grab me, and the darkness—for the time being—is left behind.

LIGHTS OUT

✛   ✛   ✛

KERNEL is already dismantling the window as I crash through and roll across the ground. "I thought we'd seen the last of you," he says as the window blinks out of existence, securing our safety.

"You wish." I grimace as I stand. I took a hammering in Lord Loss's realm, not least to my face. That was fine when I had the magical energy of the demon universe to tap into. I could numb the pain. But back on Earth I feel like I've been run through a meat processor.

Shark groans as he pries the remains of the snake from his flesh. Blood gushes from the hole it leaves. Timas makes a tourniquet out of his belt and tightens it around the ex-soldier's arm.

"I never liked snakes," Shark wheezes. "Now I bloody hate them! I'll have nightmares about that."

"You don't have enough imagination for nightmares," Kernel laughs, slumping beside his friend. He runs an eye over me and frowns. "Are you going to be OK?"

"Yeah," I mumble, coughing up blood.

"The left side of your head looks like it's been caved in with an iron."

"Thanks for pointing that out."

"I could take you to a hospital, but I doubt they'd be able to do much for you."

I wave away his concerns. "I'll be fine. A short rest, then we'll go somewhere magical and I'll patch myself up."

"She was a vindictive little wench, wasn't she?" Timas says cheerfully, as if discussing a cat who'd shown her claws.

"I'd have drowned her if I'd known what she was going to turn into," Kirilli snarls. "She saved me on the ship when we first met. I thought she was kind. But she murdered those people as if they were ants."

"We've lost her," I sigh. "She belongs to Lord Loss and Death now. We'll have to kill her the next time we meet."

"You think you can?" Kernel asks quietly.

"Over there, no. But here, where they're weaker? We stand a chance."

Silence falls as everyone thinks about Lord Loss, Bec, Death. We know we're done for. I can see it in their eyes. We can talk the good talk all we want, but the demons are stronger than us, even on our own turf. Winning is a dream, not a real possibility.

Kirilli lets out a deep breath and chuckles wryly. "We left Moe behind. I'll miss that dumb hairball. He might have thought of me as lunch, but I had a soft spot for him all the same."

"There's only one of the original werewolves left now,"

I nod. "Assuming Larry hasn't been killed." I glance at Kernel. "How long have we been gone?"

He shakes his head. "I'm not sure. But it's too long, no matter what." He backs away from me, his expression changing. "You know what I'm going to say."

"You want to leave?"

"It was madness, staying when I did. I have to go."

"You're our secret weapon," I tell him, knowing it's a waste of breath but feeling like I should go through the motions. "With your help we can make sneak attacks, dart in, strike, nip out again. If you abandon us, they'll grind us down."

"They'll grind you down regardless," Kernel sighs. "And you're forgetting, my eyes are no good here. They're already starting to sting. A day or two and they'll be gooey blobs again."

As I'm trying to think of some fresh way to argue with him, Kirilli clears his throat. "Why don't we ask for help from the Old Creatures? If they told you the truth, they have the power to hold the demons back. If we put a strong enough case to them..."

Kernel shakes his head. "They're looking at the bigger picture. Earth is just another world, one of untold billions. They don't care about us. They only want my part of the Kah-Gash."

"We could barter," Kirilli says. "What if you promised to help them, but only if they reinforced Earth's defenses? They used lodestones to deter demons in the past. Surely they could recharge or replace them and erect a ring of magic around the planet through which the Demonata couldn't cross."

Kernel looks uncertain. "I think Death has changed things. I don't know if the old ways work anymore."

"But we could ask," Kirilli presses. "If they say no, we haven't lost anything. There's no harm putting in a request, is there?"

I seize on Kernel's hesitation. "Why not try? Even if they turn you down, they won't punish you for asking, will they?"

"Probably not," Kernel says. "But..."

"What?" I snort. "Afraid of upsetting them? Will you condemn the rest of us just to make a good impression on your new friends?"

Kernel's face stiffens. "That's a cheap shot."

"Maybe. But it's not an unreasonable request. Take us to the Old Creature who came back with you. Let us discuss it with him. If he turns us down, at least we'll have tried. You can go; the rest of us will stay. Where's the harm in that?"

Kernel shrugs. "I'm sure he'll reject you, but I guess we might as well try. Let me open a window to the demon universe, then I'll—"

"Why do we have to go there?" I snap suspiciously.

"It will take several hours to open a window to Atlantis," Kernel says. "My eyes might not last that long here. Plus it's easier for me over there."

"OK," I growl, but edge to within striking distance in case he's trying to con us.

✠ Kernel takes us to a few different worlds, trying to find a spot where our enemies can't track us. Eventually, on an asteroid in the depths of space, he sets to work on building a window to Atlantis, the world where the Old Creature is waiting. Far from being a mythical country that sank beneath the waves, Atlantis is the nearest inhabitable world to Earth. It was once populated by advanced beings. They mastered space travel and visited our planet, influencing mankind's early progress. Then there was some kind of meltdown, like a nuclear war but worse. The Atlanteans perished.

I'm not looking forward to meeting the creature from the original universe, older than time itself. They're obviously a superior species, and Kernel thinks they're much wiser than us, that we'd be crazy not to follow their plans. But by their own admission they've messed up before. I don't have the same faith in them that Kernel has.

Even if the ark they've built is the only hope for survival in the future, how can they turn away from the needs of the present? The Old Creatures told Kernel they believe every species has to follow its own path. They protect us in our formative years, hold back the Demonata so that we can develop. But then they withdraw, leaving us to fend for ourselves or perish at the claws of the demons.

What the hell kind of thinking is that! If I had their power, I'd never abandon a world. The Old Creatures won't live forever. They say they can *only* hold back the demons for a few billion years. Like that's nothing! A billion years is an eternity for most civilizations. If they spared us the agonies of the Demonata that long, by the time their power waned, Earth would be a shell of a planet anyway. They could save us all this suffering.

I know they have other worlds to think about. The universe is teeming with intelligent beings, and Earth's just one small rock among billions. But if we were worth helping in the first place, they should have seen the job through. To me it's the same as if a parent teaches its child to walk, then drops it into a pit of snakes and says, "You must prove yourself worthy of survival. Good luck!"

I've all sorts of bones to pick with the Old Creatures. But I'll have to hide my feelings, smile big, and play it humble. Because these guys are our only hope. If we can convince them to help, maybe the Demonata can be driven back. I might even avoid the future that Juni prophesied and not destroy the universe. It will stick in my throat, but I have to play up to these cold, ancient life-givers. If I don't, we're on our own, and that will truly be the end.

Temper, Grubbs, temper!

It's taking Kernel ages to open the window to Atlantis. He works hard, sweating with the effort, but apparently there's no quick way because of the distance involved. When I asked him how far away it was, all he said was *far.* We can't get closer to it in this universe either—space doesn't work the same way here. Kernel has to construct a window that links back to Earth, then on to Atlantis. I'm glad I'm not the eyes of the Kah-Gash. Having to deal with technical issues like this would drive me mad. I'm much happier gutting demons.

The rest of us patch up our wounds while we're waiting. Shark and I are the worst, battered all over. The brace around his stomach has cracked in several places. He glues it together with magic, but I get a glimpse of the flesh beneath. It's ugly—purple flesh speckled with a moldy green fungus. There's blood soaking into his trousers, and bits of his guts are poking out of ragged holes.

"How much longer do you think you can keep going?" I ask.

Shark shrugs. "I should have been dead weeks ago, as my doctors kept telling me. Having cheated death this long, who knows?"

"Has the infection been there long?"

"Who made you a nurse?" he scowls.

"*Infection?*" Timas barks. "You were supposed to tell me if you got infected."

"It slipped my mind," Shark says drily.

"Let me see," Timas says, reaching for the brace.

"Leave it," Shark grunts. "I used magic to heal myself. I'll be fine." He sighs. "You know what I miss? The ladies. No matter how bad things got, when Meera or Sharmila was with us, I always felt more at ease. Crazy, huh?"

"If they were here now, they'd march you to a hospital and have that infection looked at," Timas huffs.

"Why don't you go find a machine to tinker with?" Shark snaps.

"Over here?" Timas replies archly.

"I thought *I* was supposed to be the highly strung one," Kirilli murmurs, and we all laugh.

"Seriously," Timas says, smiling, "that infection will kill you if we don't have it treated."

"Seriously," Shark responds, grinning tightly, "I know it will, but I don't think it's the sort of infection any doctor can treat. Just let me battle on and drop when it's my time.

I don't have much longer whether I push on or go back. I'd rather die fighting than tucked up in a hospital bed."

Timas considers that, then nods. "As you wish."

Kirilli chuckles. "That's the one plus point about not having any women around—we can discuss these things logically. No woman would let Shark get away with reasoning like that."

"Our kind of women would," Shark disagrees. "Sharmila and Meera knew the score. They wouldn't have objected. Or wept. They were tough."

"Yeah," I sigh, thinking of Meera on her motorbike, red hair streaming behind her, laughing as she tore past speed signs.

Silence settles over us again as we brood about the friends we've lost, the wounds we've endured. It's a relief when Kernel finally opens a window of white light and staggers away from it, exhausted.

"About time," I grunt. "Let's go."

"Wait a minute," Kernel stops me. "This is a window to a distant place in our universe, not a passageway between realms. It doesn't work like a normal window. It'll take several minutes to cross and there isn't any oxygen. The Old Creature gave me a piece of a lodestone to use."

Kernel digs out a sliver of rock and studies it. "I'll use its power to erect a shield, but I'm not sure it will hold us all. If the shield starts to crumble while we're crossing, I'll have to cut the rest of you loose."

I stare at Kernel suspiciously. "If this is some kind of trick..."

"No trick," he insists. "I wasn't supposed to bring others back with me. I don't know if I can swing it."

"Can't we erect shields of our own?" Shark asks.

"It's a different type of magic. You won't be able to tap into it."

We gaze uneasily at one another. Shark, Timas, and Kirilli wait for me to make a decision.

"Will there be any fighting?" I ask.

"On Atlantis?" Kernel shakes his head. "No. A few of the slug creatures might attack, but we can easily repel them."

"Then I'll come by myself. The others can stay here. We'll pick them up on our way back—or *I'll* pick them up if I return alone," I say quickly, before Kernel launches into another of his I-won't-be-coming-back spiels.

"You're sure you'll be safe without us?" Shark asks.

"Yeah." I grab Kernel and settle my fangs close to his throat. "If Window Boy gives me any trouble, I'll chew through his carotid artery before he can blink."

"Charming," Kernel sneers, then creates a tight, invisible barrier around us, and we shuffle into the window of light.

✠ Crossing has always been instantaneous, like stepping from one room to another through a doorway. Not this time. I find myself floating through a weird zone of lights, all sorts of shapes and colors. I cling to Kernel like a child to his father, ogling the lights, feeling completely out of my depth. I try to ask a question, but no sound comes from my lips.

"We could speak normally," Kernel's voice says inside

my head, "but it would mean more work on the shield. It's easier this way."

"Bloody telepathy," I grumble silently, then nod at the lights. "Is this what you see all the time?"

"These are different from the normal lights," he says. "But they're similar."

"How do you concentrate on normal stuff?"

Kernel laughs. "For me this *is* normal. The only time I was unable to see lights was when I entered the Board in Lord Loss's palace."

"How are we moving?" I ask. "What's propelling us?"

"I'm not sure. I think the lights draw us on. As long as I bear Atlantis in mind, they steer us towards it."

"What if you black out or go crazy?"

Kernel sniffs. "There's no telling where we might end up."

I've never felt so helpless. At least in the realm of demons, no matter how bad things got, I was always able to fight. Here I'm relying on Kernel for everything. I feel useless. On Earth I'm a magician, a leader of werewolves. Here I'm nothing. If Kernel cast me adrift, I couldn't do anything about it.

I get tenser the farther we glide. I want to go back and take my chances without Kernel. I don't mind dying on Earth or in the demon universe. But not here, in this unnatural zone of lights. It was a mistake asking him to bring me. I should have stayed where I belonged.

I fight my hysteria as long as I can, but eventually it threatens to overwhelm me. I'm about to demand that Kernel take me back, but before I can he says, "That patch of green light is the entrance to Atlantis."

I fix on the green panel and smile eagerly as we draw closer. The other panels seem to slide away from around us until the whole universe looks like one giant patch of green. Then we slip through and land on a hard floor.

We're in a chamber made of stones. The air is foul, acidic, painful to a nose as sensitive as mine. Squinting against the discomfort, I look around and spot a fat black man sitting close by. It's the Old Creature in human form, disguised as Raz Warlo, a Disciple who fought with Dervish many years ago.

"Hello, Kernel," Raz says stiffly, eyeing me beadily. "I did not expect you to bring another piece of the Kah-Gash."

"This is Grubbs," Kernel says. "He has something to ask you."

"Yes," Raz says. "I can read it in his thoughts. The answer is no."

"Hold on a minute," I growl. "You don't know what—"

"You want my help," Raz interrupts. "You want me to return to Earth, recharge the lodestones, and provide you with the means to repel the Demonata."

"Well, OK, maybe you *do* know what I want," I smile, trying to make a joke of it. "But you can't refuse before I have a chance to—"

"I can see all of your arguments already," Raz says. "None will persuade me to return with you. The threat of withholding Kernel won't work either, since he is determined to travel to the ark with me. He has a greater calling he must respect. Your world is unimportant in the grand scheme of things."

"It might not matter to you," I snarl, "but it means everything to us."

"No," Kernel says sadly. "It doesn't. I'd save it if I could, but if it's a choice between dying meaninglessly or helping others survive...I've got to go, Grubbs."

"Nobody has to go anywhere," I hiss, trying to rein in my temper. "Come with us. Give us the power to defend ourselves. You made the lodestones work once—why not again? Time means nothing to you guys. Give us a million years. That won't kill you, will it?"

"It would go against all that we believe in," Raz says. "We protect developing worlds in their infancy, but your people have outgrown the need for us. You had the power to evolve and move ahead of the demons. You failed to nurture that talent. That is your problem, not ours. If we interceded in this case, we would have to intercede in all of the others."

"What's so wrong with that?" I explode. "You have the power to save lives, to save *worlds*. Why don't you bloody use it?"

"We cannot save everyone," Raz says patiently. "The universes do not work that way. Losses are unavoidable."

"Listen to me, you ignorant son of a—"

I freeze. I'd been taking a step towards Raz, but suddenly I can't move. My hand's outstretched, one foot raised, mouth open. I must look idiotic, but there's nothing I can do about it.

"Grubbs?" Kernel squeaks, then turns on Raz. "What have you done to him?"

"Merely halted him," Raz says. "He is not harmed. When we move on, he will be freed. Come, Kernel, it is time to return to the ark."

"But he won't be able to go home," Kernel says.

"We will send him back with a piece of a lodestone to protect him," Raz promises. "He will be safe, at least until he faces the demons and is destroyed along with the rest of his kind."

"You're sure?" Kernel asks.

"I give you my word."

I want to tell Raz what I think of his *word*, but my lips are frozen along with the rest of me. I have as much control over myself as a concrete block has.

Raz gouges a bit of rock out of a lodestone, presses it into my right palm, and closes my fingers around it. Then he turns into a ball of light and starts to pulse. The stones of the chamber throb around us. Kernel casts me a shameful look and shrugs. Right now, I almost hate him more than Lord Loss or Bec. How can he turn his back on us? I might be a werewolf, but I still remember what it means to be human, and I fight for the things that mattered to me before I changed.

As I struggle to break free of the spell holding me captive, Kernel half turns and sniffs the air. His eyes narrow. He focuses on a spot a few yards away, then says, "Raz…"

"Please do not interrupt. This is very—"

"A window's forming."

The ball of light stops pulsing. "Are you certain?"

Kernel nods. "Over there." He points. "It's not one of yours?"

"No." There's a sighing sound. "How much time do we have?"

"Not—"

A window of grey light opens and Bec steps through.

"—much," Kernel finishes glumly.

Bec looks taller than before, but that's a trick of the shadows billowing around her. They encase her from head to toe, rise above her in clouds, and trail behind her like robes. Her eyes are pools of shadowy flickers. Vapors dance across her lips. The shadows move constantly, sometimes covering her completely, then parting to reveal a glimpse of her pale face. There's something of Juni Swan about her, but she looks more of a menace than Juni ever did.

"I can't let you leave, Kernel," she says, and there's the same flat tone to her voice that I noted before. She doesn't sound evil, merely determined. There's even a hint of sadness mixed in somewhere, as if she's sorry she has to do this.

"How did you find us?" Kernel mutters, backing away from her.

"I'm the memory of the Kah-Gash," she says. "I remember everything I see or absorb. When we were in contact, I shared your recent memories. I can't see the lights but I can mimic your actions and go where you've gone, and also where the Old Creatures took you. I can go *everywhere* you've been. I can even find the ark."

"No!" Raz gasps, sounding more human than he did before.

"Yes, my ancient friend." Bec smiles thinly. "You hid it masterfully, but your hiding place has been exposed. I will lead the demons to the ark and set them loose on the creatures you have gathered. Without Kernel, they're doomed."

With a shriek, the ball of light shoots at Bec. She laughs and swats it aside as if it were a fly. As Raz smashes into the wall of the chamber, his spell over me shatters and I regain control. I launch myself at Bec and land on her back. I bare my fangs and snap at her neck, but the tendrils of shadow thicken around her and send a wave of electricity shooting through me. With a choking noise, I'm flung against the wall like Raz.

"You cannot fight me," Bec says calmly. "I am two now. Death has joined with me. I am its vessel and mouthpiece. When you attack me, you attack Death—and that is a foe no one can defeat."

Raz recovers and throws himself at Bec again. This time the ball of light engages with the shadows surrounding the small girl. The air fills with high-pitched crackling noises, so shrill that blood trickles from my ears and nose. There are blinding flashes and disorienting blackouts. Bec stands immobile at the center of the warring forces, fingers twitching but otherwise motionless as the spitting shadows swirl around the pulsating ball of light.

I try to wade in, but the air close to Bec is hotter than I can stand. I get to within a couple of yards of her, then the hairs on my arms catch fire and I have to retreat and roll in the dust to quench the flames.

Kernel's staring at the battling pair, jaw slack, eyes wide. "We have to help!" I roar, staggering to my feet, wiping sweat and blood from my face.

"We can't," Kernel whispers. Blood is seeping from his ears and nose too.

"There must be something we can do," I snarl, shaking him roughly.

"Like what?"

"Unite our magic. Hit Bec hard. Unleash the Kah-Gash."

"Are you mad?" he scoffs. "Bec's part of the Kah-Gash, but now she's also part of Death. If we join, we'll link up with the Shadow. Do you want to put the power of the Kah-Gash in Death's hands?"

I stare at Kernel, then at the waves of shadows writhing around Bec. Maybe this is when I make the move that damns the world. Perhaps this is how it ends, with me handing Death the force it needs to reduce everything to ash. If it gains control of the Kah-Gash, it can use me as a puppet, pull my strings as it's jerking Bec's, send me to Earth to wreak havoc.

"We have to get out of here," Kernel pants, dragging me towards the window of green light, which is still open.

"What about Raz?" I growl, breaking free.

"He's lost," Kernel says. "It's over. Bec knows where the ark is. She can find it. The plans of the Old Creatures are ruined. Raz can't help us now. Nobody can."

"Then let's die here," I say softly, and Kernel pauses. I search his bright blue eyes for acceptance. "If this is the finish, let's go out with a bang. You and me, alone against Death. What do you say?"

Kernel licks his lips. His features soften and I think he's going to agree. I ready myself for the final battle, looking forward to the relief of oblivion that failure and death will bring. But then Kernel shakes his head.

"I don't want to die so far from home. If we can't make a difference, let's at least perish on our own world, not on a dead planet."

I sigh heavily, accepting the fact that relief isn't to be mine just yet. Nodding, I edge to the window of green light with Kernel, but stop there and study the warring giants. I don't want to quit until the fight's been decided. If Raz can surprise his foe and chalk up an unlikely victory, there's still hope.

But it soon becomes clear that victory isn't to be ours. The snakes of shadows rip into the heart of the ball of light, tearing chunks out of it. The dislodged scraps drift through the air like bits of plastic, then crinkle away to nothing. There can be no doubt that Raz is going down for the three count.

"Go, Kernel," the ball of light whispers. "You can do no good here."

"I'm sorry," Kernel moans.

"I regret it too," Raz says. "We tried so hard to prevent this, but it seems our efforts were in vain. Please forgive us. If we could..."

Whatever he was about to say is lost in a terrible screeching sound, like two huge metal plates being scraped together. There's a flash of light so intense that for a few seconds I think I've been blinded, and fire breaks out all over my body. As my sight returns and I thrash at the flames covering me, I see dozens of shards of light floating through the air. They're all that remain of the Old Creature.

The shadows settle around Bec, and her head moves, eyes following one scrap of light to another, watching with grim satisfaction as they blink out. She blows on one that drifts close to her mouth, laughing softly as it catapults through the air.

Kernel grabs my arm and makes a wheezing noise. The flames didn't take hold on him—one of the advantages of having no hair—but there are ugly scorch marks across his face, and a hole in one of his cheeks where the heat burned through his flesh. He tries to drag me away, but I pull against him and lock eyes with Bec.

"I'll kill you before this is over," I vow.

Bec shakes her head. "No."

"I'll rip your head from—" I begin, but she cuts me off.

"The fight with the Old Creature drained Death, but it's recovering swiftly. If you don't leave now, it will destroy you, seize all three pieces of the Kah-Gash, and claim victory early."

"Like you care what it—"

"Get the hell out of here, fool!" she screams, and the fear in her eyes hits me harder than any threat. With a heavy heart, I wrap an arm around Kernel and dive through the window of green light, roaring with rage and frustration, knowing all is truly lost.

TUNNELING THROUGH

✣   ✣   ✣

SHARK, Timas, and Kirilli are waiting for us on the asteroid, sitting close to the window, talking in low voices. They don't spot us immediately. It's only when Kernel groans and staggers away from me that their heads shoot up and they leap to their feet.

"Well?" Shark barks hopefully, figuring Kernel's return must be a positive sign.

"We're sunk," I tell him, and the hope flickers out in an instant.

"The Old Creature wouldn't help?" Kirilli asks.

"No. But even if he had, it wouldn't have mattered. Bec followed us. She's in league with Death. They crossed shortly after we did and killed the Old Creature."

"What are you talking about?" Shark frowns. "Kernel's the only one who can build a window that quickly."

"Not anymore," I chuckle mirthlessly.

"You mean she could come here at any moment?" Kirilli

gasps, eyes flicking from one stubby outcrop to the next, searching for unnatural shadows.

"No," Kernel says. "She can't see the lights. She said she could only mimic what I do, and go to the places I'd been to when she touched me and absorbed my memories. She can't track me."

"Thank heavens for that," Kirilli smiles.

"She can find the ark," Kernel tells him. "She'll lead the demons there."

Nobody looks unduly upset. It's hard for us to care about the ark. Earth's in trouble. People we know and love are going to die. So what if some spaceship trillions of miles away faces the same threat? Our world is what matters most. To hell with the rest of the universe. We can't think that big.

"What happens now?" Timas asks as Kernel and I sit and stare at the dead landscape of the asteroid. "Are you going to return to the ark?"

"I wouldn't be able to find it," Kernel sighs. "Bec has a perfect memory, but I don't. The Old Creatures guided me there and back. I don't know how to locate it by myself."

"Well, it's an ill wind that doesn't blow anyone a bit of luck," Shark beams. "I guess that means you have to come back with us now."

"For all the good I'll do," Kernel grumbles. "Maybe I'll just stay here and wait for the universe to end. It'd be a lot simpler."

"But nowhere near as exciting." I stand and shake blood from my face, using magic to heal the damage to my ears and nose. I don't feel depressed. I have a sense of destiny clicking into place, of things playing out the way they were always meant to. We've tried every angle we could think of and they've all failed. We've passed the point where we can save the day with a cunning plan. We're puppets of fate now. There's no use worrying about events we can't control.

"Where next?" I ask cheerfully.

Nobody meets my gaze. They don't have any ideas. We had targets to aim for up to this—Juni Swan, the Shadow, Lord Loss, the Old Creature. Now all we can do is return home, put up a good fight, and accept annihilation with a rueful grin.

"We could...," Timas says, then falls silent.

"If Bec is part of Death, and we kill her...," Shark begins.

"There are other Old Creatures...," Kirilli murmurs.

"Kernel?" I cock an eyebrow.

The surly teenager shrugs. "It doesn't make any difference."

"Then take us to Prae Athim," I decide. "If I'm going down fighting, I want to go with my faithful pack behind me."

�֎ We find Prae, a few units of soldiers, and my enhanced werewolves battling demons and a bunch of zombies outside a small town. We fall in beside them, surprising and delighting Prae. No time to exchange pleasantries. I howl at the werewolves, letting them know their leader's back. They happily return the howl and fight with renewed vigor, keen to impress.

Larry breaks away from the carnage and loops around me, snapping with excitement, sniffing me all over to ensure I'm the real deal, not some demonic doppelgänger. I bark a few commands to the last survivor of my original pack, telling him to stop sniffing and get back to fighting. As he bounds away, calling others to his side, I focus on strays around the edges and pick them off as they try to sneak away. I don't care whether they're demons or zombies. Some of the others have a hard time slaughtering those who were once living people, but they're all the same in my wolfen eyes.

It doesn't take long to bring the demons and zombies to their knees. The pack had control of the situation before I arrived. My presence merely speeds things up. Within minutes we're relaxing on a mound of mutilated corpses, cheering because it's what you do to celebrate a victory, even though it's just one small triumph in a doomed war.

"Didn't expect to see you again," Prae grins. "It's been hell here. I thought you'd fallen on some far-off demon world."

"Not a hope," I smile wryly, running an eye over my pack, noting the new arrivals, yapping at some of those I recognize from before.

"What's been happening?" Shark asks, and Prae quickly brings us up to date. Earth's in a lot worse shape than when we left. Six weeks have passed. Windows are opening at a rate of four or five a day. Demons are having their wicked way in most countries. The Disciples, mages, werewolves, and soldiers have been fighting doggedly, but I see desolation in Prae's eyes. When we left for Lord Loss's realm, people still had hope. Not any longer. From what Prae tells us, realization has set in across the globe. Even those who've avoided contact with the demons know they're living on borrowed time. They go through the motions, but without any real expectation of victory.

The zombies came from nearby. Prae says hundreds of them — and even more demons — are massed outside a city a few miles away. A lodestone must be buried somewhere close. Once Bec located it, the demons set to work, assisted by one of their treacherous mages, and opened a tunnel. Hordes of demons pushed through with vicious glee, and the dead have been coming back to life to help them.

There's a strange magical energy in the air, which Kirilli recognizes from when he fought the Shadow on the ship. Death used that energy to reanimate the corpses, and it's pulled the same trick here. The blank-eyed zombies are driven by a force they have no control over, killing recklessly, slaves to their ever-hungry master.

The first clusters of walking dead clawed their way out of crypts and graves, but many of the people killed by the demons have also been brought back to life. A lot of victims are ripped to shreds by overeager demons, but those who are left largely intact are revived by the magic of Death.

"We haven't been able to get close to the mouth of the tunnel," Prae sighs. "So we've been trying to pen them in, to stop splinter groups like this one from spreading. The demons aren't particularly strong, and the zombies are no more powerful than ordinary humans. If this tunnel is a one-off and we can hold them here, it won't prove too much of a problem."

"It's just the first of many," I tell her. "More will open and in time stronger demons will cross."

Prae nods slowly. "I guessed as much, but I still…you know…hoped."

"Forget about hope. We don't have time for such fantasies." I cast an eye over the dead around us, then peer at the city in the distance. Planes circle overhead, dropping bombs. Teams of soldiers and mages are dotted around.

"Call off the planes," I growl at Prae, starting towards the city.

"You're going in?" she asks.

"Yes. I'll find the lodestone, destroy it, and that'll be that."

"But there are a *lot* of them. More crossing all the time. They're not especially strong, but there are so many…"

"All the more for me to kill," I chuckle, then break into a jog, howling for my werewolves, leaving the humans to retreat or follow as they please.

✠ Carnage. Bloodshed. Mayhem. We cut our way through the ranks of demons and zombies, dismembering, disemboweling. Kernel guides us, tracing patches of light to the location of the tunnel. I've assigned five of the toughest werewolves — including Larry — to serve as his bodyguards, although I don't think he really needs them. Kernel was never the ablest fighter, but he lays into these opponents with determination, using magic to liquefy them or make their heads explode. I've never seen him so bloodthirsty. I guess a lot of people will be acting this way now that we're close to the end. Desperation tends to make humans act unnaturally. But if they all fight like Kernel, that will be a good thing.

Our opponents fall like bowling pins, overwhelmed by the raw force we strike them with. They kill a few soldiers and werewolves, even one or two mages. But their successes pale in comparison to ours, and it's clear within minutes that we outpower them.

They make their final stand on the outskirts of the city, where the lodestone rests in an excavated ditch. Some of the smarter demons retreat through the tunnel, back to the safety of their own universe, but most crowd around it and defend it to the death. I don't think they do so out of loyalty—they're simply too dumb to know when they're beaten.

I gut a boar-shaped demon, spit out entrails, and shoulder my way forward. Then I'm on the stone. It's an unremarkable piece of rock, set in the mouth of a small tunnel. I peer over the top of the lodestone and see a woman behind it, joined to the stone by her chin, parts of her body scattered all around, still functioning.

The woman snarls at me and says something in a foreign language. I could use a spell to translate it, but why bother? I'm sure it's more of the same old crap.

I ball my right fingers into a fist and crush the woman's head. Apart from her agonized squeal, this has no effect. Several demons throw themselves on me, but I flex my muscles and swat them aside. Then I lash at the rock with my fists, one punch after another. It cracks on the fourth blow, splits on the fifth, then crumbles after a few more.

As the lodestone breaks, a wind rips out of the tunnel. It quickly picks up speed and sweeps across the land, gathering all the demons and zombies, knocking over some of the humans and werewolves too. Using magic, I root myself and watch as the wind is sucked back up the tunnel, returning its catch to the realm of the Demonata. A few human and wolfen innocents are taken too. I can't say I'm too bothered. This is a tough world and it's getting tougher. Only the strong are worth caring about.

As the wind drops, the tunnel closes, and rocks and earth grind together. I glance around at those who remain. Many were knocked over and are picking themselves up, weeping and groaning. Prae has been clinging to a werewolf. She lets go and staggers away, then hurries to check on the rest of the pack, showing that odd maternal concern that she reserves for these hairy misfits.

"That wasn't so hard," I grin at Kernel. His eyes are wild, darting this way and that, looking for something else to kill. "Easy, big guy," I calm him, laying a firm hand on his shoulder. "It's over for now. We can rest awhile."

"Rest?" he sneers. "Don't be a child. There's another tunnel. I can smell it."

"Where?" I growl.

"The other side of the world. We can be there in minutes. You game?"

"What's it like compared to the one we just shut?"

"Bigger. It's only been open a few hours, but already more demons have come through there than here. Stronger ones too. A lot nastier than these familiars."

"Are there Disciples on the scene? Mages? Soldiers?"

"Who cares?" Kernel hoots. "I'll take them on by myself if you're chicken."

"You want to be careful who you taunt," I snarl.

"Don't be ridiculous," Kernel smirks. "You won't harm me. You need me. I'm your quick way in and out of the madness."

I eye Kernel warily as he works on opening a new window. I don't like this new, wilder version of Cornelius Fleck. Something switched off inside him when the Old Creature was killed. He thought he had a greater purpose, that he was going to save the universe. Now he's been reduced to the same level as the rest of us, scrapping to salvage an unremarkable planet on its last legs. The demotion hit him hard. I'm not sure how many brain cells he's operating on. In this state he could do anything.

But there's no time to try and help the borderline-crazy Kernel. Because even as I'm worrying about him, the window opens and he darts through. I have no option but to call my pack of werewolves to my side and push on after him, before I lose him to an army of demons and the walking dead.

BIGGER, BETTER, BADDER

✠   ✠   ✠

I know straightaway that we're in trouble. When you fight
as often as I do, you develop a knack of swiftly judging the
course of a battle. To any normal person, this would look
no different from the war zone we came from, a group of
humans and werewolves up against demons and reanimated
corpses.

But looks are deceptive. The magical energy in the air is
much thicker than it was outside the city. That's good for us,
but even better for the demons. It means stronger monsters
can cross, beasts who can channel the energy and wreak more
havoc than the creatures we crushed a few minutes ago.

There are already some mages and soldiers on the
scene. We wade in beside them, werewolves running wild,
Disciples unleashing bolts of magic, soldiers firing concentrated bursts, shredding the bodies of weaker demons and
zombies.

A group of the undead are clustered around hundreds
of screaming people. I scatter them with a wave of magic

that rips most to pieces. "Fight or get the hell out of here!" I bellow at the humans, then grapple with a massive demon that has several heads and more arms than I can count. It tugs and snaps at me, piercing my flesh in dozens of places, focusing its largest mouth on my face.

I roll across the ground with the demon, punching savagely, biting at anything that comes within range of my fangs. I drive a fist into its stomach and feel around for guts to yank out. Before I can finish off the beast, a foul stench fills the air. Looking up, I spot Kernel vomiting over the demon. As the last drops drip from his lower lip, he touches the vomit and it flashes, becoming acidic. The lethal puke sizzles through the demon's shell and it falls away, squealing with agony.

"You love that old vomit trick," I grunt, getting to my feet, wiping slime, blood, and some of the remains of Kernel's last supper from my flesh.

"It works," he says, looking for his next victim.

"I could have dealt with the demon myself," I tell him.

"I know. But I didn't like its face."

He whirls away, scanning the masses for another face that doesn't take his fancy. He certainly has plenty to choose from. I fry a few more demons, then push after Kernel. I'm worried he might do something stupid in his wired-up state.

We fight desperately, more demons crossing all the time, each wave stronger than the last. I haven't sensed any demon masters hitting the scene, but these are certainly A-plus students. They slaughter soldiers for fun, and don't have too much hassle dispatching werewolves or mages either. We've already suffered severe casualties, and the battle is only minutes old.

I force my way through a pack of zombies and grab Kernel. "The lodestone!" I yell in his ear. "We have to destroy it. We can't take much more of this."

"It's over there," he shouts, pointing to his left.

I stand on my toes. All I can see are demons and zombies, a few hapless humans trapped among them. "How far?" I ask Kernel.

"A mile, maybe more."

"How are you at flying?"

"Never tried it on this world," he says. "But I'm game."

Linking hands, we jump high. I've flown once before, with Beranabus, when he dragged me out of a plane. I've tried to repeat the trick a few times since, but there was never enough magic for me to tap into. Now there is, and we soar forward, shooting over the heads of the warring forces like a couple of blow-ins from *Peter Pan*.

Some of the more powerful beasts fire at us as we flit by. We easily deflect the balls of energy and rocks. But as we get within three hundred feet of the tunnel, a squadron of winged demons flaps into the air. We draw to a halt and eye them warily.

The demons, thirty or forty of them, hang in the air above the lodestone. They're deliberately positioned, an aerial guard to protect the tunnel.

"There are others on the ground," Kernel says sullenly. "More powerful than any we've faced so far."

"Can we take them?" I ask.

"Maybe." He casts an eye over the demons behind us. "But we'd have more fun if we tackled that lot."

"This isn't about fun," I growl.

"Of course it is," he laughs. "You taught me that. We've lost. All that remains is to take as many demons down with us as we can, and have a blast killing them."

I scowl, but I can't refute his statement. If Kernel has become a suicidal, kill-crazy goon, it's because of what I've done to him.

"Let's try for the lodestone," I mutter. "If we slip past the guards and destroy it, this will be a victory to savor."

Kernel considers that, then nods. He swoops ahead of me, issuing a challenging cry to the winged demons. With a curse, I tuck my chin down and fly after him.

The dogfight is short and vicious. The demons aren't just airworthy—they're powerful too. We try to zip through the gaps between them, but they're faster than us and more naturally suited to midair maneuvers. We hit them with balls of energy and acidic, projectile puke, but although we cause damage and kill a few of them, most shrug off our blows and respond with ear-splitting shrieks, six-foot-long talons, and beaks that can rip a head clean off a neck.

Within a minute we know it's a hopeless task. I catch Kernel's eye, shake my head, and peel away. He follows, deciding he'd rather not be pecked to death by a pack of demonic harpies. They don't chase us but settle on the ground, ready to launch another defense of the lodestone if threatened.

"I told you we shouldn't have bothered," Kernel says sulkily.

"How long can they keep that tunnel open?" I ask.

"Do I look like I'm an expert?" he huffs.

"I know you are — you've boasted about it often enough. How long?"

Kernel chuckles, then focuses on the area around the lodestone, studying the patches of light that are invisible to the rest of us. He sighs. "It won't crash any time soon. I reckon it can be kept going for a few years."

I feel sick. I take a couple of deep breaths, clear my thoughts, then turn and stomp away.

"Where are we going?" Kernel asks, tucking in behind me.

"To signal a retreat."

"We're going to run?"

"Can you think of another course?"

"Not really, no."

"Then shut up and help me pull back as many survivors as we can."

✠ We summon soldiers, mages, werewolves, and civilians, then help them fight their way clear. We lead them to a convoy of trucks and buses that is waiting a few miles away, set in place by a forward-thinking general in case the battle went poorly. The demons chase heatedly, eager to chalk up more kills before we slip through the net. Some of the faster monsters target the convoy and clamber over the roofs of the vehicles, breaking in, causing high-speed crashes. A few perish in the flames, like the humans they targeted, but most walk away, laughing, lugging severed heads, maybe to settle down over a few mugs of blood later and compare kills with their comrades.

Kernel, Shark, Kirilli, and I do what we can to minimize the damage. The others look to us for guidance, since we're the most powerful and experienced. We guide the trucks and buses to safety, repel the demons and zombies, spread ourselves as widely as possible. But ultimately we're just four guys. We can't save everyone. The losses are horrendous, in the high thousands. And they'll get worse once the demons stabilize and branch out.

When we've led the troops to safety, we head for a makeshift camp where scores of medics are tending to the wounded or setting aside the dead. I howl a few times, calling the remaining werewolves to my side. When sixteen—all that appear to be left—are gathered around me, I march to a large, vacant tent. Timas joins us along the way, responding to my howls as the werewolves did. He looks drained, and he's covered in blood splatters, but he doesn't seem to have been injured. Some soldiers try to waylay us to ask for instructions, but I wave them aside, telling them I'll confer with them shortly.

We sink into chairs in the tent and I look around wearily. Larry isn't one of the sixteen werewolves, and there's no sign of Prae Athim either.

"If you're looking for Prae, she's dead," Timas says before I ask. "She perished trying to protect a wounded werewolf. I cut her head off and incinerated it, so she won't be coming back as a zombie."

I process the news, then ask, "What about Larry?"

Nobody answers. I doubt if anyone cares. To be honest, I find it hard to work up much sympathy either, not when so many thousands have been killed. Sorry, Larry. I hope you died well, but tough luck if you didn't.

"What now?" Kirilli asks. I've never seen him look so miserable, but it's not the type of self-pitying misery he once wallowed in. He's sad because of what he's seen.

"We try to pen them in," I sigh. "Hit them with all the missiles we can. Drench the land around the tunnel with a circle of gasoline. Light it when they try to push out—fire will kill a lot of them if we add magic to the flames. Establish a perimeter of mages. Fly in volunteers, test them for magic, set new mages to work with the others. Make another assault on the lodestone when we have support."

"How far can they travel if they break through?" Kirilli asks. "On the ship, they were confined by a bubble of magic. Is there a similar bubble here?"

"No," Kernel says. "The energy from this tunnel streams out freely. There's a limit to its reach, but that might be a few hundred miles in all directions."

"Then we need to evacuate everyone within a two-hundred-mile radius," Shark says. "I'll talk with whoever's in charge, set soldiers on the job, turn this into a no-man's land."

"You don't understand," Kernel says. "We can't control this."

"You just said there were limits," Shark growls.

"To *this* tunnel, yes," Kernel snaps. "But there are more powerful lodestones. I'm sure they'll open a new tunnel soon, one of unlimited energy. The demons who cross will be able to go anywhere. And masters will be free to cross too, hundreds of demons as strong as Lord Loss, if not stronger."

"Can't we stop it before it opens?" I ask.

Kernel tuts. "I don't have a magic wand. I can sense a tunnel as it's opening, usually in advance. We can be on the scene within minutes, but what if they open two at the same time? Three? More? Demon masters *will* establish a toehold. If we weren't able to break through the defenses of this mediocre lot, what sort of hope do we stand when we're up against the real deal?"

There's a long silence. Slowly, each of them turns to look at me, placing the burden on my shoulders, leaving me to make the fatal call. I don't blame them. I'd pass the buck too, if I could. But if the buck has to stop here, so be it.

"Get your soldiers to move out the survivors," I tell Shark, "then come back. We'll rest up. Kernel will watch for tunnels. When another like this one is due to open, we'll contact those close to it and give the order to retreat. There's no point fighting the stronger demons. We'll tell everyone to run. The fast will survive. The slow..." I shake my head.

"We're not going to try and help them?" Kirilli whispers.

"We'll save ourselves."

"For...?" Shark asks.

"The big guys." I crack my knuckles. "That's my plan. We ignore the smaller, weaker tunnels. We summon the most powerful Disciples and mages, then wait. When a permanent tunnel opens, through which demon masters can cross, we hit with everything we have. If we close it, we relax and wait for the next one, then go through it all again. If we fail, there's no plan B. We triumph or perish."

"Our last stand," Timas murmurs.

"It's come to that?" Shark asks quietly.

"Yes."

"Good!" he booms, thrusting himself out of his chair. "I hate pussyfooting around. I'll pass on the word, then grab some shut-eye. Make sure you call me in time for the big show—I don't want to miss this one."

Then he strides out of the tent, leaving the rest of us to smile ruefully, wait nervously, and prepare as best we can for the end of the world.

À LA MOSES

✠   ✠   ✠

FOUR days of waiting. We're all restless and itching to go into battle. It would be easier to join one of the many wars raging around the globe than sit here and twiddle our thumbs. But as bloody as the battles are — we see and hear all about them on the constant news reports — they fall short of the apocalyptic mark. Six tunnels have been opened, but all are limited, and though millions of people have fallen to the demon invaders, the world struggles on.

I spend most of the time with my werewolves. I prefer their company to that of humans. I don't have to think when I'm with my wolfen pack, merely growl every so often to keep them in line. I lead them on occasional forays into demon-controlled territory, so they can pull out a few zombies to snack on. But apart from those welcome diversions, we mostly rest from the sun in a tent, relax beneath the moon at night, and pant and scratch a lot.

I don't have much contact with the others. I've seen Shark and Timas going from one meeting to another with a variety of politicians and army officers. They're putting some sort of emergency campaign together, acting like we have a plan, trying to keep panic to a minimum.

Kernel and Kirilli have gathered an army of mages and Disciples. They've two hundred or so lined up and ready for action. Many refused to answer their call, preferring to fight the demons who've already crossed, defending areas and people close to their hearts. Kernel and the ex–stage magician run the volunteers ragged, testing them in every way possible, toughening and sharpening them for the mother of all battles. I don't think it will make any real difference, but if it keeps them occupied, I guess it serves a purpose.

Finally, when I'm about to go stir-crazy, Kernel sticks his head inside my tent. "It's time."

I snap to attention immediately. "A new tunnel's opening?"

"Yes. Not too far from where you used to live. On the coast."

"It's the big one?"

He nods soberly. "Massive. It hasn't opened yet, but already the lights are going crazy, even from this distance."

"Tell the others," I mutter, the many hairs on the back of my neck rising. "And Kernel?" He stops and looks back. "It's been nice knowing you."

He smiles bitterly. "No, it hasn't," he says, and goes to summon the troops, leaving me to ready the werewolves for what will probably be our final fight.

✠ Kernel creates a window of orange light and we step through onto a grassy cliff. The tunnel is being opened in a cave beneath, but we wanted to get all of our troops assembled on this side before facing our foes. I stride to the edge of the cliff as the rest of the mages, Disciples, and werewolves cross in orderly file. We didn't bother bringing soldiers—they couldn't do anything against the more powerful Demonata.

It's a wild stretch of coastline, the water dashing against the rocks far below, a sharp drop to a quick, messy death. Rain falls steadily and winds rip in off the ocean, which stretches as far as I can see. The land is barren all around. I doubt if anyone ever lived in this beautiful but desolate spot.

I feel magic building in the air. It's almost the same as being in the demon universe. I let animal-shaped streams of steam trickle from my fingertips and watch as they dissolve in the rain. There are thudding vibrations from deep underfoot, as if goblins or trolls were hammering drums in the bowels of the earth, in preparation for battle.

Shark and Timas have been holding a hushed conversation. Now they move away from the cliff and Timas takes up position, partially sheltered behind a jutting rock. He's brought a stack of laptops with him and quickly sets them up. Shark stabs a few umbrellas into the earth and opens them over the technical genius to provide him with cover. Curious, I amble across to see what they're up to.

"This isn't the time for video games."

Timas looks at me gravely. "No game."

"We had an interesting debate," Shark grunts.

"What sort of a debate?" I frown.

"About the future of the planet and what happens if we lose today."

"And?" I cast a troubled eye over the laptops.

"My way of reckoning," Shark says thickly, "is if we get creamed, the people of Earth are better off dead than left to the vicious devices of the Demonata. We got clearance from most of the relevant authorities, but it wouldn't have mattered if they'd objected. Timas could have cracked the security codes."

"*Maybe*," Timas mutters. "Not definitely. It would have been an intriguing challenge, but one that it is better not to have to face."

"What are you talking about?" I snap.

Shark taps a small camera set in the shoulder of his uniform. "Several of us are wearing cameras like this. Timas will be watching. If the demons get the better of us, he has orders to press the button."

"What button?"

"The nuclear button," Timas says softly.

I gape at him, then at the grim-faced Shark. "Are you trying to wind me up?"

"Don't be a child," Shark snarls. "You said it yourself — this is our last stand. If we fall, the planet falls. I'd rather it fell to us than them. Quicker, cleaner, more humane. And we might take some of them with us."

"But..." My head spins. Maybe this is what Juni foresaw. Perhaps Timas won't be able to push the button, and the task will fall to me, and that's how I'll destroy the world.

"What's the alternative?" Shark asks. "Let the demons run free, torture and kill at their leisure, make slaves of those they choose to spare? We saw what happens to prisoners in

Lord Loss's castle. Do you want your friend Bo Kooniart to have to suffer that again?"

"We don't have the right to make this call," I whisper.

"Of course we do," Shark says. "But even so, we ran it by the watchmen of the nuclear community. There were a lot of dissenters, but a few gave us the green light, enough to make our job a formality. Timas is hooked up to bases across the world. If we run foul of the demon army, he'll bring this planet crashing down around us. There won't be a cinder ball left by the time he's finished. Let's see the Demonata get a kick out of that!"

I stare from Shark to Timas, then nod slowly. "But only if we definitely fail," I tell Timas. "Don't press any buttons just because you *think* we're going to lose. As long as one of us stands, keep your finger clear. Understand?"

"Affirmative," Timas says, then sticks out an arm. As we shake hands, he says, "Give them hell, Grubbs."

"And all the toppings," I promise, then turn my back on the Pied Piper of nuclear destruction and pray he isn't called upon to play the world to its doom.

Kernel's waiting for me. "It's open," he says simply.

"How do we get down?" I ask.

"There's a tunnel beneath the waterline. We jump and swim."

"Don't be ridiculous," I sneer. "You march bravely into a lion's den—you don't *swim* to it."

"You have a better suggestion?" he responds icily.

I stroll to the edge of the cliff. It's a straight drop to where the waves roll in and crash against the base. The easiest way, as Kernel suggested, would be to drop and use magic to protect ourselves. Under normal circumstances, that would be our only option. But there's so much energy in the air, we can be creative, like in the demon universe.

The memory of an old story comes to mind and I grin. Raising a hand, I gesture to the water below. It begins to bubble and spit. Then, as curious Disciples and mages gather around me, the waves part and an avenue opens, a stretch of dry land at the foot of the cliff, surrounded by towering walls of water.

"Hark at the modern-day Moses," Kirilli says jealously. "If I could have done that in my act, I'd have been bigger than David Copperfield."

"You ain't seen nothing yet," I drawl, then point my other hand at the cliff. With a low, rumbling sound, a thick chunk of rock a hundred feet to my right grinds out of the wall, forming a step twenty-five feet long, ten feet wide, a foot high. I cock a finger, and another chunk of rock slides out of the wall just beneath it, another beneath that, and so on. A staircase swiftly forms, reaching all the way down to the ocean floor.

"Will they hold?" Kirilli asks, eyeing the steps nervously.

"Only one way to find out," I grin, then jump off the cliff and land on a step ten feet below. It doesn't even shudder. "Hurry up," I call to the others. "Last one down's a rotten egg."

They laugh, then trail down the staircase after me to the cave where the monsters are lying in wait.

THE MISSING LINK

✤ ✤ ✤

WE creep down the stairs. Nerves fray the farther we descend. I sense a few of the mages lose their resolve and retreat. I don't pause to berate them. This isn't a place for the weak. We're better off without cowards.

That's harsh, the voice of the Kah-Gash murmurs. *It's not so long ago that you would have run too.*

"Here for the big party?" I grunt cynically. "You must be loving this."

What makes you think that? It sounds genuinely surprised.

"This is what you want, isn't it, an excuse to unleash your full power and destroy the human universe?"

If I wanted that, the Kah-Gash says witheringly, *I would have made it happen a long time ago. I wouldn't need to wait for an* excuse.

"You mean you want to destroy the demon universe?" I frown.

The Kah-Gash sighs. *You still don't understand. I don't*

want *anything. When there was only one universe, I had a natural urge to keep it as it was. Since it splintered, I have simply enjoyed the experience of being. I have no vested interest in the result of the battle about to take place. I'm merely a curious observer.*

"But Kernel said you maneuvered us into place. According to the Old Creatures, you kept Bec's soul intact when her body died. You chose to inhabit three humans at the same time. You set this up."

Guilty, the Kah-Gash chuckles. *But it was the fascination of watching what happens that motivated me. I have no yearning for one outcome over another.*

"So will you help or hinder us?" I press.

Neither, the Kah-Gash says.

"In that case, shut up," I snarl.

As you wish, the Kah-Gash whispers, and falls silent.

"Slow up, big guy," Shark says, tapping my shoulder. I glance back at him. He points to a spot behind us—the mouth of a tunnel. "That's the way to the cave. You missed it. I guess your thoughts were elsewhere."

I smile ruefully. "You could say that."

Kernel and Kirilli are waiting on the step by the opening in the cliff face. The Disciples who have come with us are on the steps above, flanked by my pack of werewolves. The mages are scattered across the steps behind. Most are trembling. A few are physically sick. But all hold. There'll be no more deserters today. Those who remain are in this until the awful, apocalyptic end.

"A few words, perhaps?" Kernel mutters.

I shrug, then face my troops and roar, "Let's kill some demons!"

With a relieved cheer—I don't think anyone was in the mood for a long speech—the mages, werewolves, and Disciples sweep after me into the tunnel. Bidding farewell to sunlight and the world of humanity, we enter the demon-riddled den.

✠ The tunnel is narrow but eight feet high. The floor is damp and littered with fish and other creatures of the sea, a few of which still flop or slither about. It's hot, the heat coming from the cave ahead of us. It's a dry, unnatural warmth that I've felt many times before, always in the presence of demons.

Kernel is beside me. He's created a ball of light, which trails us like a faithful hound. His sharp blue eyes have lost their crazed sheen. He looks nervous now.

"Stick close to me," I tell him. "We stand a chance if we fight together. Don't hold anything back. We can't worry about the Kah-Gash betraying us. We have to throw everything we can at this lot."

"What about Bec?" Kernel asks. "Do we kill her or try to link up?"

"Kill."

"There's no way we can subdue her, make her power work for us?"

I grimace. "We can try, but I'm not holding out much hope."

"I wish Beranabus was here," Kernel sighs.

"He couldn't make much difference if he was. It's you and me now. The others are for show, to make us feel like we're not alone. But we are. It all boils down to how much damage we can wreak with two-thirds of the power of the Kah-Gash."

"Do you think it will be enough?" Kernel asks.

"We're about to find out," I mutter, and with a few long strides I step into the cave of the Demonata.

It's massive, far bigger than I imagined. There are large stone pillars set in a ring around it, a few dozen or more. One of the larger stones serves as the mouth of the tunnel to the demon universe. A human—I can't tell if it's a man or a woman—has joined with it, and I see body parts mixed in with the rock. The tunnel stretches far behind, a mix of stone, flesh, and guts, veins running along the sides like railway lines on a map. Enormous demons lurk within, poised to cross. I catch glimpses of tendrils and fangs. They're crawling through the tunnel, which is still widening. It isn't ready to grant them access to this world yet, but in a short while it will stabilize and they'll pop out like mutant babies from a monstrous womb.

On this side of the divide, Lord Loss awaits us. Because he once hosted Bec's part of the Kah-Gash, he can cross freely between universes. He bobs up and down in the air close to the rock, extended arms waving gently, snakes hissing softly in the hole where his heart should be. His dark red eyes are dilated, and his lips turn down in a sad frown.

Beside him, shrouded in shadows, stands Bec. She's wearing a shawl of webs that falls to just beneath her knees. The small girl looks even more of a threat than Lord Loss, a result of the strands of shadows revolving around her and the dark, inhuman swirls in her eyes.

"So we come to this," Lord Loss murmurs as the rest of our troops spill into the cave and fan out.

"One chance, Bec," I growl, ignoring the demon master. "Come back to us and we'll forgive you. Stand against us and you'll die along with the rest of the scum."

"You know nothing of the ways of Death," Bec says quietly. "I cannot die. Even if you destroyed my body, my soul would thrive. Death will claim you today and all who come with you. And I will serve as the vessel through which it operates."

"It's not too late to change your mind," Kernel says, his voice cracking.

"Of course it is," Bec says with a thin smile.

"Then let's finish this." I howl at my werewolves and they lunge at Bec. I focus on Lord Loss. As I race towards him, roaring madly, the mages and the Disciples crowd after me, each making the choice whether to target the girl or the demon.

As I close in on Lord Loss, I leap into the air and grab hold of the cold, clammy skin around his throat. I dig my fingers in, snarling into his face, closer to him than I've ever been. He laughs as my thumbs search for his vocal cords and find only doughy flesh. His arms whip around me, the snakes in his chest bite for my heart, and we whirl through the air as if dancing.

"You cannot know how I have longed for this moment," Lord Loss purrs, his mouth no more than an inch from my left ear. "I hate you as I have hated no other human. Your death will afford me more pleasure than—"

I send a ball of energy shooting through the demon's chin and into his brain. Fire flares behind his eyes, and his flesh turns an ugly purple color. With a gasp, he half releases me and shakes his head. Loosening a hand, I aim for his eyes, but he catches me by the wrist and bends it back, tutting mockingly. His eyes and flesh regain their normal color and he smiles as I fail to unleash another bolt.

"Naughty Grubitsch," he teases. "You should play fair. But you always had a problem doing that, didn't you? On the chessboards...in Slawter...in the cave where your brother died. You never had the courage to face me honestly."

I bellow in answer, becoming more of a werewolf, searching for the strength to break free of his hold. All of a sudden he releases me and I drop to the ground. As I lunge back to my feet, I spot Bec repelling my wolfen pack with ease, slitting their throats, setting them afire, swatting them aside like flies. Shadowy tendrils snake from her in all directions and attack the humans behind the werewolves. The shadows only have to brush softly against the cheeks or chests of most of the mages. At a single touch they topple, eyes freezing, skin turning a grey shade, dead before they hit the ground. With each murder, Bec grows stronger as Death absorbs the souls of the slain.

"Kernel!" I bellow, looking for him in the middle of the madness.

"Here," he calls, stepping forward. As I run to him, Lord Loss waves a hand at the roof of the cave. Stalactites drop from overhead. They pierce the skulls of several mages around me. I could protect myself with a shield, but instead I swipe the deadly pins aside in a display of contempt.

Moments later I'm standing beside Kernel. Our eyes meet and we nod briefly. I clutch him to me with a thick arm and level the other at Lord Loss. As magic explodes within Kernel and joins with mine, I let it channel through my fingers, and streaks of black energy hiss through the air and strike Lord Loss with the force of a volcano, slamming him back against the wall of the cave.

Lord Loss screeches as we pulp him with the power of the Kah-Gash. We draw energy from all around, even from the tunnel of the Demonata. Hope blooms for the first time in ages. Lord Loss is writhing beneath our touch. If we can do this to one so strong, we can do it to others. Maybe this isn't our last stand. It might be only the first step forward to a new, demon-free future.

"The tunnel," Kernel says through chattering teeth—like me, he's struggling to hold himself together. The Kah-Gash wants to break free of our bodies and become a sheer force of energy. "We have to close it. Forget about Lord Loss."

"Never," I growl, then smile savagely. "But he can wait a while." Closing my fingers into a fist, I sever the lines of energy streaming from them. The demon master slumps to the ground, landing in a sorry-looking heap, no longer able to float with the dreadful majesty that's proved so impressive in the past.

I face the tunnel to the demon universe. The monsters within are almost at the opening. Their faces are twisted with rage and loathing. They've seen what we've done to Lord Loss. They feel our power. They know we're going to thwart their plans.

I laugh and point at the rock. Drawing power from the

tunnel, I direct it back, willing the walls to grind shut, the rock to crumble, the tunnel to disintegrate. The fleshy walls inside the mouth vibrate. The veins throb wildly. Some explode. The demons gibber wildly as blood rains down on them. To come this close to victory, only to be denied at the last moment…excruciating!

Their demented fury delights me. Taking a step closer, I draw yet more power from the universe on the other side of the tunnel. As delicious as this moment is, I can't make it last. It's time to end this battle and move on to the next. We need never be afraid of these creeps again, not as long as Kernel and I are…

Power drains from my fingers as swiftly as it filled them. With a confused cry, my head whips round. Bec is behind me, smirking. Her right hand rests on Kernel's shoulder and she's drawing power from him, and from me through Kernel.

"Stop!" I roar, throwing a punch at her.

She halts my giant paw with a glance, her smile widening, waves of shadows crackling across her pale cheeks. "We're part of the same weapon, Grubbs," she says. "You can't unleash the Kah-Gash without my permission."

"I'm the trigger," I yell. "I can do whatever the hell I like."

I try sapping power from her, as she has from us. But I can't. The flow is one way. I can draw more energy from the air—and I do—but a third of it flows into Bec as soon as I absorb it. And while I'm fighting the shadow-wrapped leech of a girl, I can't focus on anything else.

"Kill her!" Kernel screams, kicking out at Bec. He

manages to knock her hand away, but the draining flow continues.

I turn on Bec and bare my fangs. Shadows leap from around her and dart at my eyes, momentarily blinding me. Several strands snake down my throat and I gag. Whirling away from the priestess, I spit out shadows and swipe them from my face. Kernel's shaken from my grip and goes skidding across the floor.

Bec steps in front of the tunnel and spreads her arms. "Come to me!" she cries. I think she's calling Lord Loss, and my eyes fix on the demon master. He's dragged himself back to his knees, but he doesn't look ready to rejoin the fighting.

Then I realize it's not Lord Loss she's hailing. It's the others, separated from us by the thinnest of magical veils. Before I can react, a gush of even hotter air washes through the cave. As my heart sinks, the tunnel opens and a score of demons even more powerful than Lord Loss slither from their realm into ours.

THE WINK

✠　　✠　　✠

THE demon masters are no larger or fiercer in appearance than most of the lesser monsters I've fought and killed. But their power sets the air in the cave throbbing, and the scale of it stuns me. They're way stronger than Lord Loss. I realize, as they rise and look upon us with malevolent glee, that the heartless, chess-obsessed beast is only a minor master. I thought he was a king among demons, the pinnacle of all we'd ever have to face. But in comparison with this lot, he's a novice.

As more slide into view, eager to be in on the killing, the Demonata set to work on the mages, Disciples, and werewolves. They butcher arrogantly, at their leisure, picking off individuals and crushing them like balls of paper, relishing their agony. These masters could wipe out everyone with the flick of a wrist, but they want to play with us first.

I hurl myself at Kernel and link with him. He's trembling with shock, and in his eyes I see the reflection of a similarly fearful look on my own face. But I ignore the terror and focus. Drawing power from the air again, I unleash a bolt of energy at one of the masters, a green, bulbous, putrid thing, like a leech gone horribly wrong. I hit it with more power than I struck Lord Loss with. But it isn't even nudged sideways by the blast. It glances at me with a small, pink eye and sneers.

"Oh, hell," Kernel moans.

"More power," I snarl. "We're the Kah-Gash. We can take this lot. We just need more—"

"No," Kernel says, looking around. "We need Bec."

She's by Lord Loss's side, helping him. He's hovering again. He looks furious, but shameful too. He glares enviously at the other masters. Earth has always been his private playground. He was the strongest demon who could cross, a true terror for us to tremble before. Now he's been overshadowed by these new, stronger creatures. He knew this would happen—it's what he worked to bring about—but that doesn't make his loss of status any easier to bear.

A frantic Kirilli goes up against one of the masters. He shoots playing cards at it. They pierce the demon's flesh and explode beneath its skin. Kirilli's screaming hatefully, fearfully, but with excitement too. He thinks he can beat this thing.

"Kovacs, you nutter!" I roar. "Get away from there. You can't—"

"I've got it!" he screeches, unleashing a flurry of cards, face bright red from the heat and adrenaline. "This baby's going down. It should have known better than to mess with—"

The cards halt, quiver a moment, then join and form a blade. Before Kirilli spots the danger, the blade slices across him, severing his head from his body. His head flies high into the air, and a startled expression creases his features. As he watches, still conscious, the blade splits into a scissorlike mechanism and chops his head up into halves, then quarters, then eighths. Kirilli's arms twitch for a second or two. Then his body collapses and bits of his head and brains rain down upon it.

"Tah-dah!" I croak miserably, eyes surprisingly welling with tears.

"That's the way to go," Shark yells, leaping over the mess that was once Kirilli Kovacs. He lands by our side, wipes blood from his face, and grins ghoulishly. "What's the plan, boys? How do we cream these sons of hell spawn and daughters of demon dung?"

"We don't," Kernel says sullenly, wincing at the screams of the dying.

"They're too powerful," I whisper, staring horror-struck at the carnage.

Shark frowns, then slaps us with the three fingers of his right hand. "Enough of that crap. If they defeat us, fine, but we won't give up. Figure out a way to beat this lot or die fighting. But don't stand here like fools, waiting to be fried."

With a challenging cry, he bounds away and lands on the head of a scabby demon with dozens of crablike pincers. Shark rips off a few of the pincers and jabs at the monster's eyes. He punctures a couple, but the demon has several more. With a snort, it turns its head and blows a sheet of mucus over him. Shark pulls a disgusted face, tries to wipe the snot away, then screams as the snot burns through his flesh and bones.

I try to save the ex-soldier, extending my magic to him, working to nullify the acidic snot. But the demon blocks my attempt and chortles sadistically as Shark splatters into hundreds of pieces, all of which dissolve away to a gooey mess within seconds.

I stare at Shark's remains, dazed that this can be happening so swiftly, so effortlessly. I thought if we failed, we'd go down valiantly after a brutal, gallant fight. But we're being squashed like ants. This is ridiculous. When did the rules change and why did nobody warn us?

"Bec," Kernel growls, gripping my hand tightly. "We have to grab her."

"What for?" I wheeze, face ashen, watching the demons rip the Disciples and the mages to pieces. I see the last of the werewolves die in howling torment. One of the demons picks up its carcass and wiggles it around like a finger puppet.

"We can still destroy the tunnel," Kernel hisses.

I stare at him. I'm supposed to be the one with the never-say-die attitude. When I became a wolfen half-human, I put caution aside and became a one-dimensional beast who didn't know the meaning of surrender. I should be the guy coming out with crazy, suicidal plans. But I'm frozen in place, more vulnerable and helpless than I ever was before.

"If we push Bec into the mouth of the tunnel, we can explode her and use the force of the explosion to shatter the rock," Kernel continues, impossibly composed under the circumstances. "We might die too, but at least we'll buy the world some time. And maybe we can protect ourselves from the blast, live to fight another day." He shrugs. "Either way, it's our only hope."

I nod slowly, then with more determination, regaining control. "Aye," I grunt, mimicking the dead Beranabus. "And maybe there aren't any lodestones as strong as this one. If we drive this lot back, they might never be able to cross again."

We share a look that says, "*Riiiiiight!*"

Kernel grins. "To the death, Master Grady?"

"To the death, Master Fleck," I grin back.

Then we both say together, "But not ours!"

Laughing, we dart across the cave, dodging the warring humans and demons. Kernel's feet slip in the blood and slime that covers the floor, but my claws and hairy soles are suited to gripping. I steady him and we push on at a good pace.

Bec spots us closing in on her and smiles, spreading her arms as if welcoming us home after a lengthy absence. Lord Loss straightens beside her and snarls. "You should not dare—" he begins, but we're on them before he gets any further.

I leap, using all the power in my legs, and smash into Lord Loss, sending him hurtling against the wall of the cave again. Bec tuts and turns to deal with me. She considers me the prime threat and studies me warily, forgetting about the other third of the Kah-Gash.

Kernel takes advantage of Bec's momentary lapse. He sneaks up behind her and sends volts of magic frying through her brain. She cries out and jerks away from him, arms, legs, and head spasming madly. Lord Loss gasps with concern and reaches for her. I drive a hairy elbow into his ugly face, then fall on Bec and pound her as if she was a human drum. I could pop her head like a grape if I tried, but I don't want her dead. Not yet.

The shadows around Bec respond sluggishly, feebly whipping at Kernel and me, nowhere near as effective as they were before. It seems Death limited itself by uniting with Bec. As part of the girl, it suffers if she does. It can't defend itself as ably as it could when it had a body of its own.

Lord Loss hisses savagely and throws himself at us, arms lashing out, snakes darting from his chest, spitting venom as they fly at our faces. One catches my left eye and sinks its fangs in. My eye bursts and liquid soaks my cheek. I roar loud enough to shake a house. I never thought losing an eye could be so traumatic. No wonder Kernel hated me so much after I put him through twin doses of this.

Kernel tries his old vomiting trick, hitting Lord Loss with a spray of puke that turns to acid, like the snot that finished off Shark. But the demon master has seen Kernel in action before, and he's prepared. He freezes the vomit and it falls away in a thin, brittle sheet, to shatter on the floor.

But the vomit distracts the heartless monster and buys us a couple of seconds. Steeling myself against the pain, fighting the disorientation, I grab Bec and lob her at the mouth of the tunnel. As she lands at the base of the lodestone, I leap after her. Kernel scurries along behind me, unleashing bursts of energy at Lord Loss to slow him down.

The walls of the tunnel are vibrating again. It's still widening. In a few minutes, more demons will be free to cross. I hear their excited cries echoing from the universe at the far end. I recall the army we faced when we went in search of Beranabus's soul and flash on a picture of thousands

of demons pouring into this cave, obscuring us all, forc-
ing Timas to press his button on the cliff above. Whether
nuclear bombs or the crossing demons destroy the planet,
it's definitely doomed. Unless…

I pick up Bec and stagger into the pulsing mouth of the
tunnel. She stirs in my arms, then squeals and strikes me
with blasts of fire. The flames rip up my arms and lick my
face, burning my hairs to the roots, then eating deeply into
my flesh.

I ignore the pain and focus on Bec. I feel Kernel draw
up next to me, then his magic links with mine and we pour
it into the struggling girl. I want her to explode in geysers of
flesh, bone, blood, and magic. For a moment, as her flesh
ripples, I think we're going to succeed. But then she smiles
and stops struggling. Our magic flows into her, but instead of
bursting through her, it circles within the girl, then returns
to us, stronger than before, but having caused no harm.

I try again, but although I pump more power into her
than I did the first time, it doesn't hurt Bec, just comes back
at me with interest. Lord Loss settles beside me and lays a
couple of arms across my shoulders. I glare at him, but he
doesn't strike, merely smiles wickedly.

"What's happening?" Kernel yells as more and more
energy builds between and around us.

"Time to unleash the full power of the Kah-Gash," Bec
gurgles, her teeth red with blood from the pounding she took.

"She's using us," Kernel screams, trying to pull away but
held in place by the magic that continues to build. "Kill her,
Grubbs, kill her!"

I try, but I can't focus. At least not on Bec. I sense the power fanning out, the Kah-Gash taking over as it did in Carcery Vale when it sent us back into the past and gave us the opportunity to defeat the Demonata. But things are different now. Bec's working for the enemy. There's no telling what will happen this time.

I have to stop this. The Kah-Gash is the ultimate weapon. Our world will fall, no matter what, but if Bec gets her hands on the Kah-Gash, she can annihilate the rest of the universe too. If the best we can do is deny them that victory, we'll have to settle for that.

I start to cut off the power flooding through me, to thwart Bec's plan. But just as I'm about to take my finger off the trigger, Bec catches my eye and...*winks.*

The wink unnerves me. It didn't look like a mad, victorious, mocking gesture. Bec looked like her old self for a split second. It was a playful wink, the sort you tip to a friend when you have a secret, mischievous plan. The type that says, "Trust me and play along. This'll be fun!"

It's crazy. I should stop this, as I intended. Too much is at stake to gamble recklessly. But the promise in that quick wink...the spark of humanity I thought I saw lurking behind the shadowy veils of Death...

With a desperate, confused, horrified howl, I make what's probably the worst decision of my entire life, or anyone else's. Instead of freeing myself from the clutches of Bec and Lord Loss, I draw even more power from the air, giving the Kah-Gash all the kick it needs to flare into life and wreak universal havoc.

With a sudden, sickening lurch, a ball of raw, all-consuming energy bursts from every pore of my body. Similar balls explode from Kernel and Bec. The three parts of the Kah-Gash join, sizzle in the air, then strike hard at the heart of the tunnel to hell.

Everything hits the fan.

WITH A BANG

✤   ✤   ✤

W E needed words when we previously unleashed the full power of the Kah-Gash, spells to direct it. Not this time. We've moved beyond that. Grown, matured, fused completely with the weapon. There's no pulsing sky, clouds bursting into flames, melting rocks. Instead we skip straight to the exploding-into-colors stage.

My body shreds and I know instinctively that I'll never have a use for it again. Grubbs Grady is dead and gone. So are Kernel Fleck and Bec. We're the Kah-Gash now, a bodiless force, purer than light, free of all constraints. We didn't go this far the first time. We didn't understand what was happening. We tried to fight the loss of control, the madness. Now we just swing with it, leaving our humanity behind, bursting forward at a speed I can't begin to describe.

We smash through the tunnel, the world shattering behind us, the Disciples and the mages dead in an instant, Timas on top of the cliff a moment later, everyone on Earth a second after that. The planet rips apart as Juni predicted, and I'm to blame. But I don't care. I'm caught up in the moment, crazy with power, oblivious to everything except the rush of the *now*, the *here*, the *us*.

We're in a subuniverse of billions of flashing patches of light. We careened from one to another when we entered this realm before, but now the transition is fluid. Patches join and form windows. We shoot through without pause, picking up speed, the windows becoming a blur, sucking the remains of the world after us…other planets… stars…the universe…all matter…even time itself. And not just the human universe—we take from the Demonata's realm too. Everything is sucked along in our wake.

A voice whispers, "The Crux." It takes me a few seconds to realize it was Bec who spoke. It seems our individual selves still exist on some kind of level. We're not entirely the single entity I thought we'd become.

"The Crux," Bec says again, insistently.

"Why?" Kernel asks.

"I'll explain later. Just direct us there."

"But if we go to the Crux and take everything with us…"

"Trust me," Bec says. "This is the only way. Bran hatched a plan."

"Grubbs?" Kernel asks, still uncertain.

I've no idea what's going on, what the *plan* might be, if Bec's really on our side or playing us for laughs? But what choice do we have? "Make it so," I mutter in my best Captain Picard voice.

Kernel sighs. I get the sense that we've adjusted our

position. Our speed increases, the windows becoming a buzz of white light, noise building around us, drowning everything out, making it impossible for us to talk to one another.

I have a bad feeling about this, but it's too late to stop, so I continue supplying power to the Kah-Gash. I take it from the lights and everything behind us, draining the universes dry, using energy, magic, time, and all the rest to propel us forward faster. Kernel's guiding us. Bec... I'm not sure what the spirit of the Celtic girl is up to, but I get the impression that she's busy too. Her mind seems to be focused on the flotsam behind us. She's absorbing *something* from the spiraling remains of the universes. Not energy or magic. But what else could it be?

Before I can pursue the query, a fiery ball materializes in the distance. From Kernel's description, I recognize it as the Crux, the center of all things, the place where the Big Bang happened. There was only one universe originally, sixty-four zones, half black, half white, demons in the white zones, Old Creatures in the black. No other life-forms. No time either. During a war between the demons and the Old Creatures, it exploded, creating life and the universes as we know them.

We shoot through the rim of the Crux. Kernel said it was the hottest place he'd ever been, but there's nothing hotter than us right now.

There are sixty-four giant square panels floating around the lightning-pierced heart of the Crux. Clustered around them are balls of light—the Old Creatures—and enormous demons even more powerful than the masters in the cave. These are the original Demonata, those who existed before the new universes were born.

The Old Creatures and the demons react with shock as we tear into the Crux. Panic-stricken, they try to mount a defense of the giant panels. But we swat them aside and they're torn to pieces by the trailing vortex, sucked in and ripped apart like all the others, perishing with a chorus of confused howls.

I expect us to slow to a halt, but instead we carry on at full speed, then split as we hit the center of the Crux. There's a blinding flash. We separate into sixty-four fragments and strike the black and white squares. They flare, and ripples run across their surface. Sparks shoot out of them.

Then everything clicks together. The sixty-four squares join in less than the blink of an eye. We become one again, only now we're enmeshed with the squares. We explode outwards, the squares expanding with us. We're the barriers between zones, but we also fill the infinite space inside them, everywhere at once.

The expansion lasts millions of years, but it's also instantaneous. That doesn't make sense, but it's the only way I can explain it. Time has shattered. The laws we lived by—that all creatures lived by since the Big Bang—exist no longer. In the absence of time, everything happens immediately yet gradually.

As I'm trying to get my head around the new laws, there's a sudden click and the expansion stops. Everything settles. The last traces of the universes I was familiar with disappear completely. The worlds, stars, people, creatures...gone. Erased from history. The souls of the dead are gone too. In this universe, their bodies never existed, so their souls never developed. All is undone.

Before I can go insane with guilt, I notice beings blinking back into existence. The Old Creatures and the Demonata who were alive when Bec, Kernel, and I became the Kah-Gash are revived and returned to their proper places in the universe. The dismayed Old Creatures pop up in the black squares and wail at all that has been lost. The delighted Demonata—both the original demons and those they sired—materialize in the white squares and go wild with joy.

Time has been eradicated. Humanity and their kind are no more and never were. The original order has been restored. Death can function as an unconscious force, the way it was meant to. Demons will live forever, breed, and kill without limits. The Old Creatures will drift along meaninglessly in their otherwise lifeless zones, or be tracked down and slaughtered by demons. The Shadow and the Demonata have won.

The end.

AH YES, I REMEMBER
IT WELL

✠   ✠   ✠

N0, you idiot, it's the beginning."

Bec laughs, and light bubbles around me. I blink and shield my eyes with a hand. Then frown. Hang on—I'm a bodiless force. I don't *have* eyes or hands.

"You do now," Bec giggles.

Lowering my hand, I stare with astonishment at the little girl sitting on a couch I know only too well. It's from my old home, the mansion in Carcery Vale. I'm in the enormous living room, in my regular spot opposite the oversize TV. Bec's sitting across from me, smirking. A confused-looking Kernel is in a seat nearby.

"What the hell..." I stop, something about my hand unnerving me. I turn it over, wondering what's wrong. Then I realize—there are no hairs. The skin is smooth and pale. The fingers are large but not inhuman, and instead of claws I have ordinary fingernails. I'm not a werewolf.

"Of course you aren't," Bec snorts. "Not unless you choose to be. You can make yourself muscular and hairy if you want, but I'd rather you didn't. You looked so silly prancing about as a man-wolf."

She gets to her feet and walks to the window. She's dressed in simple clothes, just a cloak or something like that wrapped around her. I'm in my favorite jeans and T-shirt. Kernel's wearing something similar.

I follow Bec to the window. As I cross the room, I spot objects snapping into place around me — vases, books, pictures. The room is still forming.

Bec is staring out of the window at nothing. And I mean *real* nothing. It's black out there, the pure blackness of empty space. As I watch, some of the garden from home sprouts into view and spreads, looking strange against the dark backdrop. I see Bec's reflected smile in the glass. She turns and beams at me.

"What's going on?" I mumble.

"I'm making a temporary base for us," she says. "I figured it might help us adjust more smoothly."

"And these?" I ask, nodding at our bodies. "Are they real?"

"As real as we want them to be," she says enigmatically, returning to the couch.

"What does that mean?" Kernel snaps. "Is this a dream? Reality? How are you..." He stops, head twisting from one side to the other. "I can't see the lights," he whispers.

"Of course not," Bec says. "We *are* the lights now. They were part of the Kah-Gash. Now that we've become it, you don't need to see them. We've moved beyond that stage. We're not physical beings. We don't really have eyes or ears, or even brains. You have to start thinking bigger than that."

"How about you just explain it to us nice and simply before we lose patience," I growl, flexing my fingers.

Bec laughs. "You can't threaten me, Grubbs. This body's for show. You could grind it to dust and it wouldn't make the least difference." She clicks her fingers, and her head explodes. Blood pumps from her neck. Kernel and I yelp with shock. Then a new head grows out of the stump. Her eyes open and she winks. She waves a hand over the blood on the couch and it fades.

"I don't get it," I mutter. "Is this fantasy? Are we dead?"

"No, you moron," Bec says. "We're the Kah-Gash. The universe is us and we're the universe. We're the glue holding everything together, the power that drives it, the force..." She sees incomprehension in my eyes and sighs. "Are you getting any of this?" she asks Kernel.

"I think so," he says slowly. "But..." His face drops. "We destroyed the world! The people we knew—are they all...?"

"Dead," Bec says cheerfully. "Torn to atoms, then broken down even further. None of that universe exists any longer. Time and all its creations are lost forever. In this universe they only ever existed"—she taps her head—"up here."

"I'm glad you're taking it so well," I snarl, advancing on her, trying to figure out a way to kill her, to make her pay for the awful massacre she tricked us into engineering.

"Don't be a child," Bec tuts. "I didn't trick you into anything. I tricked *them*—the Demonata and Death. It was the only way. Bran figured it out. He couldn't be certain it would work, but in the absence of any alternatives, we had to risk it."

"If you don't start making sense quickly…"

Bec shakes her head. "With such a small brain, I don't know how you made it this far." As I open my mouth to protest, she points a finger at me. "The trigger." She points to Kernel. "The eyes." She taps her chest. "The memory. You gave us the power to undo time and all its trappings. Kernel guided us. And I absorbed."

She waves a hand at the ceiling and it turns transparent. The sky above is black. Impossible to see anything. But as we watch, an object comes into focus. I'm not sure where the light that strikes it comes from, but it's fully lit and even more recognizable than the room we're sitting in. It's the moon, full-size and round, a pockmarked pearl in a sea of darkness.

"I remembered everything about the original universe," Bec says, smiling up at the lunar giant. "I couldn't access those memories, but they had to be there. If that universe was ever to be reassembled, the Kah-Gash would need the blueprints to restore everything accurately.

"Bran knew that too. It's what gave him the idea. He figured if the memory of the Kah-Gash could store everything from the original universe, it should be able to memorize all of the new universes too.

"I was busy while you two were incinerating galaxies," Bec continues. "To rip the universes to shreds, we had to touch every planet, person, animal, atom. As we touched and tore, I committed everything to memory. The whole of history, from the moment of the Big Bang to the end…it's all up here." She taps her head.

"I know the names of every intelligent being, the spots

on the wings of every butterfly that broke out of a cocoon, the genetic codes of the simplest and most complex of creatures. I know how suns functioned, how worlds formed, how life evolved. All of the secrets of the old universes are mine. They can be yours too, if you want me to share, though I suspect you aren't bothered."

"So you remember," I grunt. "So what? It's still gone, isn't it?"

"Gone but not forgotten," Kernel murmurs, his forehead crinkling thoughtfully. "Look at these bodies—they're real. Perfect replicas, down to the smallest detail. That's right, isn't it, Bec?" She nods. "And the moon is real too?"

"Exactly the way it was before we blew it to pieces," Bec grins.

"We can bring it all back!" Kernel shouts. "The Kah-Gash has the power to tear a universe apart, but it also has the power to rebuild it!"

"That's what Bran counted on," Bec chuckles.

I stare at the pair of them, still confused. "What's the point of building a fake universe?"

"It won't be fake," Bec corrects me. "It will be as real as the old universe was. We can do anything. We can make all the solar systems, worlds, and creatures the same as they were before. We'll let history unfold as it did first time around, begin with the initial sparks of life and build from there. Advanced species like humans will live and develop souls again. Everything will happen as it did from the dawn of time up to the moment of universal destruction. We'll direct proceedings that far, then give the inhabitants of all the worlds their freedom. The future will be in their hands after that."

"What's the point?" I frown. "The Demonata will wreck it all. They exist too. They'll cross and destroy, just like—"

"You weren't listening," Kernel interrupts. "Bec said we could do *anything*."

"You mean we'll protect them from the demons?" I shake my head. "They found ways to twist the laws before. That's why the Kah-Gash shattered. We can't be sure that we can stop them doing it again."

Bec crosses the room and takes my hands. Her fingers are trembling. "We won't have to protect our people if the demons aren't there," she says softly.

"But they are. I can sense them."

"I can too," Kernel says. "I know where all of them are, along with the Old Creatures. If I close my eyes, I can visualize all sixty-four zones and track the whereabouts of every living being."

"The Kah-Gash holds everything together," Bec says. "We *are* the universe. We bind every molecule to those around it. Nothing can hide from us. And nothing can defy us." The mansion fades and we're floating in space, illuminated by the light of the re-created moon. The freezing cold and lack of oxygen doesn't affect me. Why should it? As the Kah-Gash, we *create* temperature, air, all the rest. I begin to see why Bec and Kernel are so psyched.

"The Kah-Gash never sought to control the universe," Bec says. "It had no will of its own. It simply held things in place. It didn't know why it kept the demons and Old Creatures apart—it just did. It wasn't capable of making choices."

"But *we* are," Kernel says, a twinkle in his eyes.

"Ideally we should respect the order of the original universe," Bec says. "Never interfere. Let things develop in their own way. Stay neutral."

"But to hell with that," Kernel grins. "I think this is why the Kah-Gash began to explore after it split, why it took up residence in a host of different creatures. It was learning, growing mentally, choosing."

Bec nods. "Choice was everything. When the piece in Lord Loss chose to leap into me—that's when the Kah-Gash gave us the means to self-govern, assuming we could work out the kinks."

"Are you getting it yet?" Kernel smirks.

"I think so," I sigh. "We can build it all again, the worlds and people of our own universe?"

"Yes," Bec says.

"We can re-create time?"

"Or the semblance of it," Kernel says.

"But before any of that..." I close my eyes and focus. Like the other two, I can sense the position of the demons, every one of them, spread across thirty-two zones, still celebrating their triumph and return to eternal life. As the Kah-Gash, we're the force holding their bodies together, the blood gushing through their veins and arteries, the cells of their grey, lumpy brains. We bind them. But if we choose, we could just as easily...

"...*un*bind them." I open my eyes and smile. "We can wipe them out. Kill them all. Eliminate each and every one of the beasts."

"Yes," Bec says, then her features crease. "But we mustn't."

"What do you mean?" I frown.

"It would be genocide," Bec says.

"Don't be crazy," I laugh. "They're demons, not humans. It can't be genocide if you only kill monsters."

"They're living beings," Bec insists. "They're cruel and merciless, certainly, but that's just their nature. They have a right to exist."

"No, they don't," I protest. "They tried to wipe us out. Hell, they did! They never cared about our right to life. Why should we care about theirs?"

"Because we're better than them," Kernel answers softly, taking Bec's side. "If we kill them, we'll be as bad as they are."

I shrug. "I can live with that."

Bec's eyes flash and she gets ready for an argument. Then Kernel snaps his fingers and says, "Wait. I remember something. Give me a minute..."

While we stare at him, Kernel turns his back on us and hunches down. Moments later a landscape swims into place around us. We're in a valley and everything's a light blue color. There are jagged pillars all around us. It looks familiar, but I don't know why.

"This was the first place in the demon universe you came to when you crossed with Beranabus and me," Kernel reminds me. He waves a hand at one of the shorter pillars and an angular demon steps out. As I gaze at it, Beranabus forms in front of the creature. It's not the real Beranabus, or even a reconstruction, merely a recorded image of him. Bec starts to cry when she sees the magician, but they're tears of happiness.

"No," the recording of Beranabus says to the demon. "We're not going to leave you alone. You know who we are and what we want. Now..."

"I remember," I sigh. "I was surprised. I thought all demons were as powerful and dangerous as Lord Loss."

"Yes," Kernel says. "Before you left, you wanted to know why we didn't kill the blue demon."

As I nod slowly, Beranabus answers the question, as he did that first time. "Not worth killing. There are untold billions of demons. They're all evil, but most can't hurt us or cross to our world. That cretin doesn't even dare leave this valley. It waits, hiding and surviving, doing precious little else."

"Hiding and surviving," Bec echoes. "Are we going to slaughter the weak and innocent, Grubbs? Is that what we've sunk to? If it is, I don't think we should stop with the Demonata. We should destroy ourselves too. If we can't grant mercy to those who've done us no harm, we have no more right to this universe than those we've fought so hard against."

"OK," I snap. "There's no need to rub it in. I see where you're coming from. We'll leave the weak ones alone, those who can't cross, those who don't pose a threat. But the masters have to be taken out—I won't budge on that. Any beast that even looks like it has the potential to cross, to defy us, to pick at and weaken the structure of the Kah-Gash...we wipe them out now."

"We could isolate them," Bec murmurs. "Imprison them in a place where they can't—"

"No!" I bark. "They're too much of a risk. We kill every

master going. I won't bend on this one. They have this coming to them, and I'm going to see that they get it."

"We have to do it," Kernel says, trying to win Bec round. "They found a way to destroy the Kah-Gash before. They could do it again. To guarantee order, we have to remove them. It's the only way to be sure."

Bec sighs, then nods reluctantly.

"I knew you'd see sense," I chuckle, then grin viciously, the old wolfen Grubbs Grady reemerging momentarily. "Let's give them hell!"

And the massacre begins.

DEVILMENT

�   ✝   ✝

THE demon masters perish in their millions. They don't see us coming and are helpless in the face of our wrath. We sweep through the white zones like a cosmic wind, obliterating all who pose a threat. We don't torment those we kill. Unlike these vile monsters, we're not evil-hearted and don't wish to cause pain. I'd be lying if I said part of me doesn't enjoy the cull, but I don't revel in it.

Because time doesn't work like it did before, the culling is both swift and drawn out, lasting the drawing of a breath and the birth and death of a dozen suns. It happens across all thirty-two zones at the same time. We don't have to localize. We can be everywhere at once, moving across the face of a million worlds in the same instant.

We blow through the demonic zones with godlike barbarism, felling all who need to be eliminated. We don't bother with bodies or battles. We move as spirits, a force of nature, and the demon masters are crushed, never knowing what struck them, most dying without a chance to even howl in retaliation.

It's clinical and cruel, precise to a devilish degree. We rip through the white zones, staining them red, killing every demon master in existence…except one. Him we save for the end. The rest are vipers to be crushed. We go about our work dispassionately. But with the last one, it's personal. It's payback time, and I know that when I look into his dark red eyes and see the final flame of life flicker out, I'll be so ecstatic I could burst.

✠ When all the other masters have been taken care of, and only one remains, deliberately isolated and spared, we create bodies for ourselves and fade into existence outside his castle of webs. The demon is waiting for us at the edge of the moat running around the fortress, sitting on the throne that used to rest inside. He looks more alone than ever, bereft of all his peers. But not scared. He's aware of everything that's happened—I made sure he could hear and see it all, so he'd know we were coming for him—but to my surprise he doesn't look afraid.

"Welcome again, my young friends," Lord Loss says, clapping cynically. "You have grown in stature since your last visit. Your incineration of the demon masters was impressive, if overzealous. Beranabus would have approved, but I wonder if Dervish would have, or Meera Flame?"

"We did what had to be done," Kernel growls.

"I would say you did far more than that," Lord Loss counters. "The powerful masters from the original universe

I can understand. They posed a threat and always would have. But what of the lesser masters, those with powers similar to mine? You could have easily prevented them from crossing or attacking you. They posed no threat. You could have left them to patrol the depths of their realms and harm none except their own. Yet you chose to kill them too. You rained hellfire down on all."

"Because you were all as bad as each other," I snarl.

"In whose eyes?" Lord Loss asks. "Yours?"

"Yes."

He smiles mockingly. "Who gave you the right to pass judgment on an entire species, Grubitsch Grady?"

"No one. I took it."

"How *demonic* of you," Lord Loss purrs.

"If you're trying to make me feel guilty, you'll need to do better than that," I sneer.

"I doubt if I am required to sow the seeds of guilt," he murmurs. "Eternity stretches ahead of you. Given time, I believe your conscience will torment you of its own accord."

"He's boring me," I yawn, glancing at the others. "You ready to kill him?"

"Yes," Kernel says eagerly, taking a step forward.

"Wait," Bec mutters. Her cheeks are flushed and she's staring at her feet.

"You don't feel sorry for him, do you?" I ask incredulously.

"No," Bec says.

"You can't feel any loyalty," Kernel half laughs. "I know you played the part of his servant, but it was only an act." He pauses. *"Right?"*

Bec looks up and takes a deep breath. "We struck a deal," she says, and I groan.

"What sort of deal?" Kernel frowns.

"Never mind," I snap before Bec answers. "We're killing him. That's final. I don't care what was agreed between the two of you. Dervish, Bill-E, my mum and dad, Gret... all dead because of *him*. He perishes like the rest of his foul kind. No argument."

"We can't kill him," Bec says miserably. "I hate him too. He killed people close to me or caused their deaths. But you saw us enter the Board together. We made a deal. If I don't honor it..."

"What was the deal?" Kernel asks again.

"No!" I roar. "I don't want to know. He's a demon. We don't owe him anything. I'm going to kill him, and if you try to stop me, I'll—"

"Kill her too?" Lord Loss pipes up, relishing the conflict.

"Enjoy the show while you can," I snarl, raising a hand to obliterate him.

The universe tightens around my fist, and it falls limp at my side. I whirl on Bec, fire in my eyes.

"The Kah-Gash can be split again," she says. "If we fight with each other, we risk everything. Our sacrifices and endeavors will have been for nothing if we bicker and lose control. All that we knew and loved will be truly lost then."

I count to ten, reining in my anger. Then, through gritted teeth, I say, "Tell me about the damn deal."

"He helped us," Bec says. "I told him of Bran's plan to let the Demonata build a tunnel and break through, then use the Kah-Gash to tap into the power of the tunnel and take time back to its very beginning."

"Lord Loss knew we'd kill all the demon masters?" Kernel gasps.

"Yes," Bec says. "He thought we'd kill the familiars too. He didn't believe I could persuade you and Grubbs to spare them."

"And you let us go ahead?" I spit at the demon master.

"Why not?" he murmurs. "They meant nothing to me. A vile, beastly lot. The universe is better off without them."

As Kernel and I gape at Lord Loss, Bec explains. "My betrayal was a charade. I slaughtered the souls in the Board, but I knew we'd have to kill a lot more than that if we were to triumph. We can bring them back to life later, the same as all the others.

"We tricked Death and the Demonata. Convinced them I was on their side, that I wanted to live forever as one of them. We needed Death to work through me, so I could control and subdue it when the Kah-Gash was reunited."

"But if Death was part of you, didn't it know what you were planning?" Kernel asks.

Bec shakes her head. "It didn't have access to my inner thoughts, only those I chose to share with it. Death was new to consciousness. It had a lot to learn about the mind." She smirks. "I guess now it never will."

"I protected her from my savage brethren," Lord Loss says. "I helped bring the three of you together and did what I could to ensure you were not killed before you had the chance to join. It was a risk, of course, but a calculated one, and in the end it proved to be enough."

"But why?" I croak. "You're a demon. You hate us."

"Not at all," he retorts. "I adore mankind. I'd have happily strung *your* guts out for cats to play with, Grubitsch, had things worked out differently. But humans... the games you invent... the sorrows you suffer..." He smiles at the memories.

"What do you get in return?" Kernel asks. "What did Bec promise?"

"My life," Lord Loss replies. "And a promotion." He looks at the stars twinkling far above us. "I was never as powerful as you believed. You realize that now, having seen and exterminated much stronger masters than me. I was a young, humble demon. That's why I focused on Earth. I knew I could impress there, that if I made it my personal playpen, I could dominate the human realm of fear."

"You chose to be a big fish in a small pond," I snort.

Lord Loss tilts his head. "Stronger masters terrorized galaxies, inspiring horror across a multitude of worlds. I lacked that power, so I concentrated on a single planet. I tested several before I chose Earth. Your people appealed to me, for reasons I cannot put any of my fingers on. Perhaps I was guided by the Kah-Gash. Maybe even then it had selected your world to serve as its dramatic stage."

"You're pathetic," I sneer, seeing my old foe in his true colors, astonished that I lived so long in fear of him, considering him the worst of any imaginable enemy.

"I was," Lord Loss says calmly. "No longer. I am the last demon master, the final sentinel of sorrow. All of this universe's demonic familiars must bow to my power now. I'll also cast a dark shadow across the hearts and minds of the creatures in your universe, weaving my web of misery across more worlds than any master ever came close to before. I'll be the source of every nightmare, the face behind each malicious mask of myth. I'll sow fear everywhere my eye alights, and reap the rich rewards for all eternity."

"What makes you think we'll let you?" I challenge him.

"Bec promised," he smiles.

I cock an eyebrow at the girl.

"We need him," she says quietly. "Every developed world had its boogey men, evil spirits, devils. The universe requires a force of evil for the wicked to gravitate towards, a malevolent being that the dark-hearted can worship. If they can't turn to Lord Loss, we'll have to play that hideous role. I don't want to be a monster to the twisted and the vicious of our own worlds. Do you?" she asks me. "Or you?" she throws the question at Kernel.

Kernel and I look at each other uneasily.

"Why him?" I grumble. "We can bring back one of the others that we killed, or use a familiar. It doesn't have to be Lord Loss. I want to destroy him. After all he did to us…"

"They do say, 'Better the devil you know,'" Lord Loss murmurs slyly.

"I gave him my word that we'd let him rule the white zones," Bec says. "Plus, he vowed never to overstep the mark, to leave the Old Creatures alone, to cross only when authorized and always return to his own realm when his work is done. He won't establish toeholds in the human universe, or allow his familiars to settle there either."

"But the familiars won't be able to cross universes this time," Kernel frowns. "We'll stop them."

"We can't," Bec says. "History demands their presence. If we're to let time unravel as it did before, every demon crossing will have to be recreated. I'll work in tandem with Lord Loss, letting him know when and where his familiars should cross. When we reach the present—the time when we ended the universe—we'll set him free to operate by himself as long as he respects the rules, and at that point we can put a stop to the crossings of lesser demons. Our people can be free of the monsters after that, but not before."

"How can we trust him?" I growl.

"I gave my word," Lord Loss says stiffly. "I have always honored a promise."

I shake my head. "We're better off without him. We can control and direct the familiars by ourselves. Lord Loss would be a threat. We'd have to watch him like a hawk."

"No," the demon master says. "That's merely an excuse, Grubitsch. You wish to kill me to exact revenge. You cannot justify my execution any other way."

"Then I won't," I shrug. "I'll kill you and take your place. I'd rather that than let you carry on. You're the reason I'm here, the cause of everything bad that ever happened to me. If it wasn't for you, my parents would be alive, Dervish and Bill-E, all the others. I won't spare you, not after the hell you've put me through. I'd rather burn."

I raise a hand to wipe out the demon master. I'd meant to torment him before I finished him off, but now I'll settle for a quick kill.

"Your words hold the key to my reprieve," Lord Loss says calmly as I point a finger at him. His self-satisfied smirk infuriates me, but for some reason I can't bring myself to strike. "If not for my interference, you wouldn't have joined with Kernel and Bec. The Kah-Gash could never have been utilized as it was. All has been shattered to be rebuilt, but if not for *my* actions, it would have simply been destroyed.

"I put you through hell, yes, but it was a hell you *needed* to experience. The pain, suffering, death...all were necessary. I served the purpose of the universe, just as you did. If not for my dark presence, you would never have found the path you were required to travel.

"People need devils and dark gods, if only to give them a foe to rally against, an obstacle to overcome. Your people understood that there can be no light without darkness, no good without evil, no triumph without setbacks. You can't kill me because I'm part of all that you are, all you've done and plan to do. You don't have to like me. You can even loathe me. But you must accept me."

I tremble with frustration. Part of me wants to whip him down, wipe that smirk from his face, kill him no matter what. But everything he says rings true. I owe it all to him, the good as well as the bad. As despicable as he is, he set this in motion. It wasn't intentional, and he acted selfishly at every turn, but if Beranabus was right and some godly force in our universe chose heroes and molded them, maybe Lord Loss was part of the *über* plan, as vital a player as Bec, Kernel, or me.

"I'll be watching you," I snarl. "If you take just one wrong step..."

"Why should I?" he smiles. "I never yearned to conquer your world, Grubitsch, merely to revel in the torment of its many desperate souls. Now I will become the pit of darkness at the center of the entire universe, a web into which all the weak, helpess, and vindictive must fall. What more could I wish for?"

"I hope you choke on it," I sneer, then let my body unravel and return to my ethereal state. The last thing I see through my human eyes is Lord Loss rubbing his eight stumpy hands together, leering eagerly, awaiting the dawn of time and the birth of the first of the billions whose misery he'll wallow in like the ugly, heartless, flaccid, but essential leech that he is.

ONCE MORE, WITH FEELING

✠ ✠ ✠

Lord Loss sows all the sorrows of the world
Lord Loss seeds the grief-starched trees

In the center of the web, lowly Lord Loss bows his head

Mangled hands, naked eyes
Fanged snakes his soul line
Curled inside like textured sin
Bloody, curdled sheets for skin

In the center of the web, vile Lord Loss torments the dead

Over strands of red, Lord Loss crawls
Dispensing pain, despising all
Shuns friends, nurtures foes
Ravages hope, breeds woe
Drinks moons, devours suns
Twirls his thumbs till the reaper comes

In the center of the web, lush Lord Loss is all that's left

START ME UP

✣   ✣   ✣

WE pick a black square at random and set about putting together the building blocks of life. The three of us work as one, without having to discuss what we're doing. Bec provides the memories, and thus the blueprints of what we need to start life again. Kernel manipulates the hidden strings of the universe to bring into being anything Bec desires. And I supply the power, channeling the energy of the Kah-Gash through them.

It's a long, complicated process, yet at the same time swift and simple. This is what the Kah-Gash does. It's like a person breathing, walking, talking, snapping his or her fingers. As humans we performed countless natural functions every second of the day. This is the same, only on a cosmic level.

The Old Creatures are aware of what we're up to, and we can sense their seal of approval, even though we never communicate. They're happy to drift along in their own zones. All they ever wanted was to be left alone, safe from the threat of the Demonata, to roam as they pleased. We can guarantee that now, so they have no further interest in us.

I wish we had it so easy. There are hard times ahead. Having to focus for billions of years...put worlds, ecosystems, and civilizations back the way they were...ensure every seed finds the egg it was meant to...guide every animal from a single-celled organism upwards, on every planet, in every galaxy...determine the deaths of all creatures, down to the fraction of a second of the date when they were meant to die...

It's no walk in the park!

One problem we don't have to worry about is the harvesting of souls. As strong as we are, there's a higher force than the Kah-Gash. We can sense it, but we can't define it, something greater than power, knowledge, life, or death. We could give it a name, but that's not our job or our right. Let the beings of the universe name and worship the force in whatever ways they wish. We're not here to provide answers, just to give others the opportunity to marvel at the secrets of the heavens and perhaps one day unravel the mysteries for themselves.

I'm not looking forward to letting bad things happen. I'm sure I'll be tempted to intervene a million times a day, spare innocents, undermine tyrants, build a better, safer, cleaner universe. But it's a temptation I must ignore. If we start to interfere, we'll rob individuals of the right of self-determination. Nothing good can come of celestial dominance, no matter how noble our intentions. We're architects of this universe, nothing more, and we must never let ourselves forget that.

Having said that, we'll have to direct traffic up to a certain point, to the moment when we tore the universes asunder. We could start fresh if we wanted and let things develop randomly, but there's no telling what would happen then. Life might never evolve at all. We think it's better to start the ball rolling, guide the creatures of this universe along the path they followed the first time around, then withdraw and leave them to themselves.

Well...maybe we'll stop a *bit* earlier. We don't have to let time stretch to the very last second. There's no harm tying up some loose ends a day or two before the universe ended. We have to implement change at that stage anyway, fiddle with the order of events to ensure this new universe isn't annihilated. It wouldn't make any real difference if we rounded things off a week or two earlier...maybe even a few months or years...

"That's dangerous thinking," Bec notes, her voice coming from every part of the universe and yet from nowhere in particular. "We agreed we wouldn't interfere."

"But we have to at the end," I argue. "If we let events play out as before, the re-creations of ourselves will tear the universe to shreds. We have to make changes. There can be no wandering pieces of the Kah-Gash. Death must remain a force and never be unleashed as the Shadow. No war between the demons and humanity. We have to juggle events, remove a few individuals from the mix, strip some of power, give others more to do. It'll be like a game of chess. We can let the game unfold as it did before, but if we want to avoid checkmate, we'll have to readjust the pieces a few moves shy of the finish."

"That makes sense," Kernel agrees.

"So where do we draw the line?" Bec asks. "Grubbs was the last to be born. Do we set the universe free just before that? Or do we go back to before *I* entered the world and release our grip then?"

"That would be the simplest thing," Kernel says, but there's an uncertain edge to his voice.

"The trouble with stopping there," I mutter, "is that the people we knew might never be born. My parents, Gret, Dervish…"

"Shark and Sharmila," Kernel says.

"Bill-E and Kirilli," Bec sighs.

"We could keep them all," I croak. "Even save them. My parents don't have to be slaughtered. We can give Dervish a stronger heart. Bill-E and Loch needn't die in the cave in Carcery Vale."

"Shark could live to fight another day," Kernel murmurs. "We could let Nadia lead a normal life and spare her the indignity of becoming Juni Swan."

"Bran could enjoy a dignified retirement," Bec muses aloud. "Meera could be spared. Maybe Dervish would finally see sense and fall in love with her."

"We have the power," I whisper. "We need to tinker with things, no matter what. Why not make a few beneficial, personal changes while we're at it?"

"Do we have the right to alter the universe to suit our own desires?" Bec asks.

"Let's call it a perk of the job," I chuckle.

"We should discuss this further," Kernel says.

"A *lot* further," Bec adds.

"Fine," I shrug. "We've got plenty of time. I'm sure we'll sort something out over the next billion years or so." I create a giant pair of knuckles and crack them loudly. "Now let's get this show on the road. Who wants to set the Big Bang in motion?"

"That's your privilege," Bec says. "Everything's in place. Kernel and I can't do any more until you generate the explosion."

"We *can* control it, can't we?" I ask. "The Big Bang, I mean. It won't affect any of the other zones?"

"Not this time," Bec says.

"It will all run smoothly," Kernel assures me.

I'm nervous now that the moment has arrived. It's no small thing, creating life, the universe, and everything. I'm probably not the best man—hell, best *boy* for the job. But then it's not a perfect universe. You can't hang around waiting for somebody else to pull your strings. Destiny's what you make of it. You have to face whatever life throws at you. And if it throws more than you'd like, more than you think you can handle?

Well, then you have to find heroism within yourself and play out the hand you've been dealt. The universe never sets a challenge that can't be met. You just need to believe in yourself in order to find the strength to face it.

Where to start? I feel like I should say a few words to mark the occasion, but I'm not good at speeches. Perhaps I could borrow from one of the many creation myths that have been—will be—written by others more adept at capturing the spirit of momentous events like this.

I start to ask Bec if she can recommend an appropriate

extract. But then I recall something Mum used to read to me when I was young. Mum wasn't especially religious, but she read to Gret and me from a variety of holy books. I don't recall the exact way it went, and I guess my choice won't suit everyone, but what the hell, this is my show, so I'll run it the way I please.

Clearing my throat, to a chorus of good-natured groans from Kernel and Bec, I chant solemnly. "In the beginning Grubbs created the heavens and the earth, and everything was dark. Then Grubbs said, 'Let there be light!'"

And there was light.

Coolio!

THE END

THE DEMONATA
FEBRUARY 6, 2001–JUNE 5, 2009

"What's wrong?" Larten whispered.

"One of the owners was with Traz," Vur panted. "They were on their way to inspect the room of baby worms."

Word spread and everyone upped the tempo. It was bad news whenever one of the owners came to visit. Traz got nervous in the presence of his employers. He would meekly lead his boss around, a false smile plastered in place, sweating like a pig. As soon as the visitor departed, Traz would take a few swigs from a bottle of rum that he kept in his office, then storm furiously through the factory, finding fault wherever he looked.

They were hard days when Traz was on the

warpath. No matter what you did, he could turn on you. Even the most skillful workers on the looms—normally the best-treated in the factory—had suffered lashings at times like this.

Larten prayed while he worked, begging a variety of gods to keep Traz away from their vats. Though Larten wasn't religious, he figured there was no harm in covering all the angles when trouble was in the air.

They heard a roar, and every child lowered their head and dunked cocoons as fast as they could. The problem was, they had to leave the cocoons in the water until they had softened properly. If Traz found hard cocoons in their baskets, it would be far worse than if he thought they were going slowly.

Traz entered like a bear, growling and glaring, hoping someone would glance up at him. But all the children stared fixedly into their vats. He was pleased to see that most of them were trembling. That sapped some of the fire from his rage, but he needed to hand out three or four more beatings before he'd really start to calm down.

A girl lost her grip on a couple of cocoons as Traz was passing, and they bobbed to the surface. He was on her like a hawk. "Keep them down!" he bellowed, swatting the back of her head. She winced and drove the cocoons to the base of the vat, soaking the sleeves of her dress.

"Sorry, sir," the girl gasped.

Traz grabbed her hair—she was new to the team and had made the mistake of not cutting it short—and jerked her face up to his. "If you ever do that again," he snarled, "I'll bite off your nose."

It would have been funny if anyone else had made such a ludicrous threat. But Traz had bitten off more than one nose in his time—a good number of ears too—and they all knew that he meant it. Nobody snickered.

Traz released the girl. He wasn't interested in newcomers. He knew the younger children were terrified of him and probably dreamed about him when they went to bed every night. They were too easy to scare. He wanted to work on some of the more experienced hands, remind a few of the older lot of his power, make sure they didn't start taking him for granted.

He cast his gaze around. There was a tall boy in one corner, a lazy piece of work. Traz started to move in on him, but then he caught sight of Vur Horston and changed direction.

Traz slowly strolled past Vur, giving him the impression that he'd escaped the foreman's wrath.

But when he was about four strides past, he stopped, turned, and stepped up behind the boy.

Vur knew he was in trouble, but he worked on, not giving any sign that he was aware of Traz's presence. Larten could see that his cousin was in for a beating, and although he risked drawing attention to himself, he raised his head slightly to watch. He felt sick and hateful, but there was nothing he could do.

For a while Traz didn't say anything, just studied Vur as he dunked cocoons and held them beneath the surface of the water. Then he stuck a thick, dirty finger into the vat and held it there for a couple of seconds.

"Lukewarm," he said, withdrawing the finger and sucking it dry.

Vur gulped but didn't move. He wanted to throw more sticks on the fire–even though the heat was fine–but he had to keep the cocoons down. If he released them early, he'd be in an even worse situation than he was now.

Behind Vur's back, Traz scowled. He'd hoped the boy would panic, release the cocoons, and give the foreman an excuse to batter him.

"You're a vile, useless piece of work," Traz said. He tried to think of something more cutting, then recalled someone telling him that the boy was an orphan. "An insult to the memory of your mother," Traz added, and was delighted to note the boy's back stiffen with surprise and anger.

"You didn't know that I knew your mother, did you?" Traz said slyly, walking around the vat, cracking his knuckles, warming to the game.

"No, sir," Vur croaked.

"She didn't work here, did she?"

"No."

"So where do you think I knew her from?"

Vur shook his head. Across from him, Larten guessed what the foreman was up to, but there was no way he could warn Vur. He just hoped that Vur was reading Traz's intentions too. Usually Vur was a better judge of people than Larten was, but fear had a way of shaking up a person's thoughts.

"Well?" Traz purred.

"I don't know, sir."

"Inns," Traz declared grandly. "I knew her from inns."

Vur's head rose and he frowned. Larten groaned — his cousin had swallowed the bait. This was going to be bad.

"Beg pardon, sir, but you're mistaken. My mother didn't work in an inn."

"She did," Traz sniffed.

"No, sir," Vur said. "She was a seamstress."

"By day," Traz jeered. "But she earned a bit extra by night." He gave Vur a few seconds to dwell on that. "Worked in a lot of inns. I met with her many times."

Vur was too young to have kissed a girl, but there were few true innocents in the world at that time. He knew what the foreman was implying. His cheeks flushed. The worst thing was, he couldn't say for sure that it was a lie. He was almost certain that Traz was toying with him, but Vur had few memories of his parents, so he couldn't dismiss the insult as an outrageous piece of slander.

"She wasn't a pretty thing," Traz continued, relishing the twisted look on Vur's face. "But she was pretty good at her job. Aye?"

Vur started to tremble, but not with fear. He had always been able to control his temper–much better than Larten could–but he'd never been subjected to an insult of this nature before.

Traz whispered something in Vur's ear. The boy's face went white, and a lone cocoon bobbed up inside the vat.

"Keep the bloody things down!" Traz roared, punching Vur hard in the left side of his head. Vur was slugged sideways and lost his grip on the cocoons. They all shot to the top. "Idiot!" Traz yelled, and followed it up with cruder curses, each accompanied by a blow to Vur's head.

Vur tried to push the cocoons down again but was knocked away from the vat by the bullying foreman, then to the ground. As he hit the floor, Traz kicked the boy in the stomach. Vur cried out with pain, then threw up over Traz's boot.

The foreman's fury doubled. Cursing the boy with his vilest insults, he grabbed cocoons from the vat and lobbed them at Vur's face. Vur retreated like a crab, trying to avoid the soggy missiles. Larten and the others watched with their jaws open. They had never seen Traz as mad as this. Nobody was bothering with work any longer. All eyes were on the furious bully and his defenseless victim.

When the vat ran out, Traz plucked cocoons from the vat next to it. He had never before manhandled the valuable balls of silken thread, but something inside him had snapped. It wasn't anything Vur had said or done. This had been building within the hate-filled foreman for a long time, and Vur was simply in the wrong place at the worst possible moment.

Traz stamped after the fleeing Vur, pelting him with cocoons, calling the boy and his mother all sorts of disgusting names. Larten saw Vur getting close to the door and prayed his cousin wouldn't make it. He had a vision of Traz slamming the door shut on Vur, over and over, smashing the bony boy to pieces. It would be better if Vur collapsed in the middle of the floor. All Traz could hit him with then would be his fists, his feet, and cocoons.

As if responding to Larten's silent prayer, Vur stopped crawling and held his ground ahead of the advancing foreman. But Vur hadn't stopped to take a beating. Something had switched inside him, just as it had inside the vicious Traz. Vur knew it was lunacy, but he couldn't stop himself. Maybe it was a reaction to one of the insults aimed at his dead mother. Maybe a bone had shattered in his ribs and the pain drove him momentarily insane. Or maybe life had been leading him to this point since he first stepped into the factory, and it was simply his destiny to one day hit back at a world that treated helpless children so repulsively.

Vur snatched a cocoon from the floor, hurled it at Traz, and screamed, "Leave me alone, you…" He paused as the cocoon struck Traz between his eyes, then smiled and finished with an insult every bit as crude as any the foreman had used.

Traz came to a stunned halt. The cocoon had only left a wet, slimy mark behind, and he'd been called far worse in his time by drunkards, scoundrels, and women of ill repute. But no child had ever spoken that way to him. And he had never been struck in front of a crowd of gaping children.

Traz was a beastly man and always had been. But in that second he slipped beyond the boundaries of mere brutality. He had beaten children senseless in the past. He had chewed off noses and ears, and the story about cutting out a girl's tongue was true. Children had died under his watch from festering wounds and starvation, and he had laughed at their agonies. But he had never set out to openly murder one of his crew.

As the cocoon dripped on the floor and the echoes of Vur's curse died away, Traz lost control of himself. It was abrupt and awful, and before anyone knew it was coming, he had already launched himself at the boy.

Traz scooped Vur up from the floor with one huge paw. Vur cursed him again and hit him with a fist instead of a soft cocoon. But Traz was in no mood to play. Instead of beating the boy, he swept Vur over to the nearest vat and shoved a cringing girl out of his way. Before Vur could protest, Traz upended him and thrust him underwater, pushing him all the way to the bottom and holding his head there with one thick, hairy, powerful hand.

Vur kicked out wildly. One of his feet struck Traz's chin. The foreman grunted and slipped. Vur bobbed to the surface like a cocoon. But then Traz regained his balance and pushed Vur down again, using his free arm to bend back the boy's legs. Ignoring the heat of the water, he held Vur in place, fingers squeezed tight into the flesh of the boy's skull.

"Let him go!" Larten shouted, surprising even himself.

Traz's eyes flared and he bared his teeth. "Stay out of this!"

"Stop it!" Larten cried. "You'll kill him!"

"Aye," Traz chuckled. "That's what I'm aiming to do."

Larten had lived in fear of the foreman since the age of eight, but there was no time for terror on that cold, gray Tuesday. Vur was drowning. Larten had to act swiftly, or it would be too late.

Abandoning the safety of his vat, Larten raced towards the laughing Traz and threw himself at the monstrous man. The floor was wet, and he hoped Traz would lose his footing when he was tackled. If he could get Vur out of the vat, they'd flee like rats and never come back. His father wouldn't care, not when Larten told him what had happened. There were limits to what even the likes of Traz could get away with.

But Traz had clocked the Crepsley boy's every move. He anticipated the leap and adjusted his stance. When Larten threw himself forward, Traz simply let go of Vur's legs–not thrashing now–and slammed a fist down on Larten's skull.

Larten felt as if his head had been caved in. For a few seconds he came close to blacking out. He would have fainted any other time, but he knew Vur needed him. He couldn't afford to fall unconscious. So, drawing strength from deep within himself, he shook his head and lurched to his knees.

Traz was surprised. He thought he'd killed the boy, or at least hit him so hard that he'd slump around simplemindedly for the rest of his days. Even in the midst of his murderous fit, he found himself respecting the way Larten hauled himself up, first to his knees, then to his feet. His legs were swaying like a drunk's, but Traz admired the boy for rising to make a challenge.

The worst of the foreman's rage ebbed away, and he grunted. "Stay down, you fool."

Larten moaned in reply and staggered forward. This time he didn't try to hit the huge man. He was only focused on Vur's legs. They were as still as a crushed dog's, and Larten knew he had mere seconds in which to fish out his cousin—if it wasn't already too late.

Traz squinted at the advancing child. When he realized Larten was only worried about the drowning boy, Traz looked down and hissed. Vur Horston was no longer moving, and no bubbles of air were trickling from his mouth.

Traz felt no guilt, merely unease. Though he doubted his employers would care too much if word of this incident reached them, there was always the possibility that they might decide he had gone too far. Releasing Vur's legs, he stepped away from the vat and wrung water from the sleeves of his jacket, thinking hard.

Not being a man of the world like Traz, Larten thought there was still hope. He gurgled happily when Traz moved aside, then gripped Vur's legs and dragged him out of the vat. His cousin was heavier than normal, his clothes soaked, and Larten was still dizzy from the blow to his head. But it only took him a couple of seconds to pull Vur clear and lay him on the floor.

"Vur!" Larten called, sprawling beside his motionless cousin. When there was no answer, he turned Vur's head sideways and pried his lips apart to let water out. "Vur!" He slapped the silent boy's back. "Are you all right? Can you hear me? Did he—"

"Silence!" Traz barked. When Larten glanced up, blinking back tears, the foreman added coldly, "There's nothing you can do for him. The gutter rat's dead. All that's left for him now is the grave."